She wasn't the same girl he'd left behind. It seemed she was stronger for their parting.

He glanced down at his hand and flexed it. The leather of his glove creaked; his hand inside was stiff. A year ago he'd got into a car accident during a bad bout of fog on the highway. His hand had been crushed. Quinn flexed his hand again, curling and then releasing it. Yes, it had been broken, and he'd undergone countless surgeries to repair it, but he could still use it.

His hand had mended with time. Perhaps Charlotte's heart had too, in the five years they'd been apart.

He doubted it. When Charlotte had greeted him it had been so formal. So forced.

"Whoa—that was a bit rough," Quinn remarked as they hit another disturbance. He was no stranger to flying, but that was the most jarring bit of turbulence he'd ever experienced. Of course he was used to first-class seats instead of being crammed into a small cockpit beside the pilot— especially an alluring pilot like Charlotte.

His shoulders almost brushed hers in the tight enclosure. Just that near brush of her body against his sent his blood pumping. Just being in her presence again aroused him. Charlotte was a strong aphrodisiac, like ambrosia, and she tasted just as sweet too.

Dear Reader

Thank you for picking up a copy of SAFE IN HIS HANDS, my debut book with Mills & Boon® Medical Romance™. I'm thrilled to be sharing this with you.

It's always been a dream of mine to become a writer, especially with Harlequin®, and this stems from my grandmother's hidden stash of romance novels—books we shared together as she bravely fought and then lost her battle with cancer.

SAFE IN HIS HANDS was inspired by my love of northern Canada. Even though I was raised in Toronto, my family has strong roots firmly planted in the muskeg and forests of northern Ontario. It also comes from my admiration for medical professionals who work under the toughest conditions worldwide to provide healthcare.

Also, this book is about a second chance at love, because I believe there's always a second chance—especially in light of a tragedy, like the one which separated my hero and heroine years before.

I hope you enjoy my debut Medical Romance®. I love to hear from readers, so please drop by my website: www.amyruttan.com

With the warmest wishes

Amy Ruttan

SAFE IN
HIS HANDS

BY
AMY RUTTAN

First published in Great Britain 2013
by Mills & Boon, an imprint of Harlequin (UK) Limited.
Harlequin (UK) Limited, Eton House, 18-24 Paradise Road,
Richmond, Surrey TW9 1SR

© Amy Ruttan 2013

ISBN: 978 0 263 23378 0

Harlequin (UK) policy is to use papers that are natural, renewable
and recyclable products and made from wood grown in sustainable
forests. The logging and manufacturing process conform to the
legal environmental regulations of the country of origin.

Printed and bound in Great Britain
by CPI Antony Rowe, Chippenham, Wiltshire

Born and raised on the outskirts of Toronto, Ontario, **Amy Ruttan** fled the big city to settle down with the country boy of her dreams. When she's not furiously typing away at her computer she's mom to three wonderful children, who have given her another job as a taxi driver.

A voracious reader, she was given her first romance novel by her grandmother, who shared her penchant for a hot romance. From that moment Amy was hooked by the magical worlds, handsome heroes and sigh-worthy romances contained in the pages, and she knew what she wanted to be when she grew up.

Life got in the way, but after the birth of her second child she decided to pursue her dream of becoming a romance author.

Amy loves to hear from readers. It makes her day, in fact. You can find out more about Amy at her website www.amyruttan.com

This book is dedicated firstly to my husband, Chris.
I couldn't do this without you.

A big thanks to my critique partner, Ann R, who read
this book in its many incarnations and never once
complained about reading it yet again, and my editor
Suzanne Clarke who whipped my hero into shape!

Also a big thanks to a certain group of ladies, in
particular Kimber, for cheering me up every day!

And lastly a big thanks to all the physicians
and healthcare professionals who do work in
remote places because of their passion
to provide healthcare to everyone.

CHAPTER ONE

DAMN. WHAT'VE I done?

Dr. Charlotte James had been watching the arrivals board in the Iqaluit airport for some time. She was so focused on arrivals she didn't even notice the people coming and going around her. A watched pot never boiled, or so the old saying went, but she couldn't help it. This was probably the longest she'd ever stood still. In her job there was no time to stand still. In fact, she hated it. She could be doing so many other things. Filing, for instance.

Not that she particularly *liked* filing. She preferred her organized chaos. However, there were a ton of files on her desk, and Rosie had been pestering her for a week to put them away. Instead, she was waiting here for *his* flight to arrive.

"Flight 207 from Ottawa now arriving at gate three."

The past, when it came to Dr. Quinn Devlyn, was where it needed to be: firmly locked away. She'd moved on and she had no doubt his life had, too. He was, after all, at the top in his chosen specialty, and she was right where she'd always wanted to be.

This time Quinn Devlyn wouldn't blindside her or suck her into some crazy off-kilter distracting, albeit passionate, love affair.

No, siree.

Her life was good. Not perfect but, then, whose was? Charlotte was happy.

Courage.

She spun around and saw the plane taxi in on the small airstrip, blending in with the stark, white landscape of Canada's High Arctic. The only color out there was the brightly painted houses that dotted the landscape. Her pulse thundered between her ears.

He's here.

The pit of Charlotte's stomach dropped to her knees. No. Scratch that. Make it the soles of her feet. Not since her MCATs had she felt this way, as though she was perpetually on the verge of hurling.

She was seriously beginning to doubt her sanity in bringing her ex-fiancé up to Cape Recluse. It wasn't a place where she could avoid him easily. He'd be constantly underfoot and she was dreading every moment of it. Would she be able to resist him? The only time she had resisted him had been when he'd left. When their relationship had ended, she'd never wanted to see him again, but his presence here now was a price she was willing to pay to help out her friend.

Get a grip on yourself.

A blast of cold air shook her from her reverie. Her gaze focused on the tinted windows, watching the passengers head across the tarmac to the warmth of the bright yellow airport building. Immediately she picked Quinn's form out of the group of passengers.

Tall and broad, even though he was huddled down under his collar against the cold. Just the sight of him made her heart beat a little bit faster, her cheeks heat and the butterflies in her stomach go crazy. Her pulse thundered between her ears like a marching band. She hadn't seen him in five years—not since he'd walked out on her—but he was making her feel like a giddy teenager again.

Don't let him affect you like this, Charlotte chastised herself. She'd moved on with her life. The wound he'd left in her heart had finally healed.

The double doors opened and he stepped into the airport, moving to the side to let more people in from the frigid cold. He set down his luggage and unwound his scarf.

Damn, he still looks as good as ever. Charlotte had been kind of hoping Quinn's fast, career-driven lifestyle would've caught up with and aged him, but he looked as sexy and charming as ever.

Even from a few feet away she could see there was a bit of gray around his sandy-brown temples, but it suited him. Made him look more dashing and debonair. Some stubble shadowed his chin, but it didn't hide the faint line of the scar that crossed his lips. A tingle of heat shot through her body as she suddenly recalled the way his lips had brushed across hers. A flush of goose bumps spread across her skin just at the thought of the way he would kiss a path down her body, his strong hands caressing her, holding her.

What're you doing? She was not some lovestruck goofy med student anymore. She was a physician with a thriving practice. There was no way she was going to let him in again.

Hell would have to freeze over, not that it would take much, given the current temperature outside was minus thirty.

Charlotte shut those memories away firmly, refusing to think about them any further.

Instead, she remembered how he'd brushed off the miscarriage of their child as being for the best.

As a chance to move to New York and pursue their careers.

Only New York had not been what she'd wanted. She was where she wanted to be. Not to follow him had been her decision, her right to go after her dreams.

I can do this for Mentlana.

This was all for her best friend. The only thing close to a family she'd had since her father had died when she was ten. Charlotte never knew her mother, who'd died when she was two. Mentlana and her family had been there with open arms when Charlotte had returned to Cape Recluse after Quinn had left and she'd lost her baby.

Correction: *their* baby.

Now Mentlana needed help and Quinn was the best when it came to neonatal medicine. For her best friend, Charlotte would face death itself. Even though, as far as she was concerned, Dr. Quinn Devlyn was far more dangerous than the Grim Reaper. She'd take him on, anyway.

Quinn would save Mentlana's baby.

Mustering her courage and holding her head high, Charlotte strode over to him. All the while her heart was racing and her knees shook like they were about to give out on her. He looked up, his chocolate gaze reeling her in as she moved toward him. His eyes were twinkling and she suddenly remembered how easy it was to get lost in those eyes.

They were hypnotizing.

The thought frightened her and she stopped a foot away from him, frozen in fear. Distance from him would be the safest.

Remember, he left you. You can't get hurt again. You're over him.

She couldn't let her guard down when it came to Quinn Devlyn.

Not now that she was finally whole again.

"Well, well. If it isn't the great wilderness physician," he teased, as his eyes roved over her from head to toe, a haughty smile on his lips and that damn dimple in his cheek popping up.

His mocking tone made her grind her teeth just a bit. She pressed her lips together, forcing a smile. "Dr. Devlyn. I'm glad you could come."

"It's Dr. Devlyn, now? When did we become so formal? I know we didn't part on good terms, but can we drop the formalities?" The spicy scent of his cologne—a clean scent of masculine soap and something else—teased her senses.

"Fine, but first names are as far as we go, do you understand? You're here in a professional capacity. Nothing more."

"Agreed. I would expect nothing less, Charlotte."

It was the way he said her name that triggered the memory. The two of them together for the first time, locked in a small hotel room in Niagara Falls, and the way he'd whispered her name against her neck.

"God, Charlotte. I need you."

I need you. Never, I love you. She should've taken that as a sign when she'd said yes to his proposal in the first place, but she'd been so blinded by love.

Charlotte nodded, but blooming warmth in her stomach spread to her cheeks. "Did you have a good flight?" she asked, trying to make small talk.

"As good as can be expected. The man next to me seemed to invade my space a lot, but overall it was as enjoyable as any other flight." He pulled up the handle to his rolling suitcase with a snap. The tone was a bit arrogant and that attitude was why she'd never brought him to Cape Recluse when they had first got engaged. Quinn had champagne tastes and was a city slicker through and through. Of course, if she'd brought him home when they had first got engaged it might've saved her some heartache.

Then she wouldn't have lost the baby, except she didn't regret carrying his baby, even for such a short time. She had known from the get-go that Quinn was not a family man. In her youthful naivety she'd thought she could change him.

How wrong she'd been.

Let it go.

It was no longer her job to care what Quinn Devlyn thought. "Well, we'd better get up to Cape Recluse. It's a two-hour flight there and there's talk of a storm coming in from Labrador. Also, I'd like to get up there before it's dark."

"It's two o'clock in the afternoon," he said, puzzled.

"The sun sets early up here."

"I thought this was the land of the midnight sun?"

"In summer… This is winter. We have long periods of night."

"Yikes." Quinn shook his head. "So how are we getting there?"

"I fly." Charlotte turned on her heel and strode off toward the other section of the airport where her plane was kept in a private rented hangar. Quinn kept in step beside her.

"What do you mean, you fly? As in a plane?" His tone was one of surprise and perhaps awe.

"Yes, I don't have wings." To prove her point she flapped her arms. Quinn rolled his eyes; he had never been one for foolishness in public places.

"You know what I mean. When did you learn how to fly?"

"About four years ago, after a man died in my arms from a very *mild* myocardial infarction. His death could've been prevented if we'd had regular flights from Iqaluit to Cape Recluse. By the time the air ambulance landed, Mr. Tikivik was dead. It was then I decided to learn how to fly, so I could fly my patients to Iqaluit if need be."

"So you're a physician and a paramedic, as well?" The tone was sarcastic, making her bristle with annoyance. His attitude on job specifications certainly hadn't changed one bit.

"What else are they supposed to do? Plan their medical emergencies to fit around a pilot's schedule?"

"I didn't mean to upset you. I think it's a lot to ask for limited pay."

Charlotte turned to face him. "Money doesn't mean that much to me. Lives mean more."

Quinn didn't respond but looked a bit taken aback. Guilt assailed her. She didn't want to pick a fight with him, not after he'd come all this way and on his own dime.

"Sorry," she apologized.

"For what?" he asked.

"If I insulted you."

"You didn't. You have nothing to be sorry about."

"Of course." Charlotte shook her head. Quinn never had hidden the fact that success and to be the best in his field drove him. In his eyes you were nothing without those attributes.

"I'm interested in meeting Mentlana Tikivik and examining her and the baby. Still, I don't quite understand why you don't just fly her down to Toronto."

"She has a pulmonary embolus."

Quinn whistled. "Does she know about the diagnosis of the fetus?"

"Yes, I told her." Charlotte sighed. "I told her I was bringing a specialist up to determine the severity of the CCAM. She's aware of what may have to happen, and she's fine with it. She wants to do whatever it takes to save her baby."

Just like I would've done to save mine.

A lump formed in her throat as her mind wandered back to that horrible day when she'd spotted the mass on the baby's lungs. She'd recognized the congenital cystic adenomatoid malformation, or CCAM, for what it was, and there had been no way she could fix it. She was only a general practitioner. She wasn't qualified.

"Of course." He nodded. "Did you explain the procedure to her?"

"Oh, yes." Charlotte couldn't help but smile as she remembered having to go through each step of the procedure, like she was talking to a first-year surgical resident.

"Did she understand?" Quinn asked, confused.

"Eventually," Charlotte replied.

"Eventually?"

Charlotte laughed. "She understands, but Mentlana is very…inquisitive. I'll warn you now, she'll bombard you with questions."

"No need to warn me. I've dealt with worse, I'm sure. I've

consulted on many patients before and I've a way of explaining complex medical procedures so patients understand me."

Charlotte rolled her eyes. "Your pride is healthy, I see."

Quinn smiled. "I have an excellent bedside manner."

In your dreams, perhaps.

"Right, I forgot about your charming persona with patients." She snapped her fingers. "You're something of a Mc-Steamy."

"A…what?"

"Never mind, it's a *Grey's Anatomy* joke."

"Didn't that character die?"

Charlotte smirked. "I didn't know you were a *Grey's Anatomy* fan."

He sighed. "What I meant was that I have a way of getting people to open up to me. I have a winning personality."

Charlotte cocked an eyebrow. "Is that so?"

Quinn chuckled. "Okay. Look, what I meant was I'll be able to explain it to her and gain her trust. I've done this surgery before."

Trust was important, especially in the Inuk culture. Trust was important to her, too. She'd trusted Quinn. She'd never forget how deeply in love with him she'd been. Quinn had claimed her heart, body and soul. He'd taken her innocence and had then crushed all her hopes and dreams when he'd walked out on her after she'd lost their baby.

"It's for the best, Charlotte. We're not ready. We have our careers ahead of us."

The day he'd walked out had been the day he'd lost her trust. She'd never let him in again.

Never is a long time.

"Hey, are you okay? You zoned out, there, for a moment," Quinn said, waving a hand in front of her face.

Charlotte shook the painful memory away. "If you're sure you can handle Mentlana, I'll leave you to it."

"Charlotte, your friend will be totally at ease and informed during the entire procedure."

"Trust is not easily given by people in a small, close-knit and isolated community."

"Trust me." He grinned, a dimple puckering.

"I did that once before," she muttered.

"What?" he asked. He hadn't heard her, but when had he ever? When they'd been together, everything had been about him and she'd been so in love she'd been content to follow.

It had taken her a long time realize she'd been so desperate to have her own family she'd been blinded to the fact she had been engaged to a man who was already married—to his work.

"Don't worry about it." Though Charlotte wasn't entirely sure he could fit in with the residents of Cape Recluse. A man like Quinn would stick out like a sore thumb.

"Should I worry?" he asked.

"So, I was surprised to learn you're in Toronto," Charlotte said, changing the subject but also feeding her nosy side. New York had been Quinn's dream destination, his Mecca, his reason for leaving her, but when she'd called he'd been in Toronto.

"My father's health deteriorated two years ago. He offered me a position at the hospital. He wanted to groom me to become Chief of Surgery." Quinn frowned and quickened his pace. Charlotte had an inkling it was a touchy subject. At least that explained why he'd given up his practice in Manhattan and moved to Toronto. It impressed her that he'd returned home to help his father, despite his history with his parents.

"Did he retire?"

"No." His voice was stiff. "No, he died."

Good going, dingbat.

"I'm so sorry. I didn't know."

Quinn shrugged. "It was his fault. He didn't practice what he preached. Excessive smoker and drinker. Cancer caught up with him."

"Still. I'm sorry." Charlotte didn't know what else to say.

She knew Quinn hadn't had the best relationship with his parents, but it was still hard to lose one. She was practically a pro in that department.

She led him into a warm hangar where her little Citation jet was waiting. Quinn whistled in appreciation.

"Where did you get this?" he asked.

"I bought it at an auction. It's a '93 and was in bad shape interior-wise, but I didn't care about that. I kitted it out to transport patients."

"It's a beaut."

Charlotte grinned. She was proud of her jet and it made her preen that Quinn looked up at it in admiration. When they had been choosing their specialties, he hadn't been overly impressed with her choice of general practitioner.

You don't need his approval.

"Well, then, we'd better get going. I'll be back in a moment. I just have to clear something with the hangar's manager."

Charlotte jogged away. Quinn's personality was the same: overconfident, arrogant and cocky. But none of that mattered right now. His self-assuredness would probably be just the thing needed to save Mentlana and her baby.

And that was all that mattered.

What am I doing here again? Quinn asked himself, as another round of turbulence rocked the plane. Yet he knew exactly why he'd come. Because of Charlotte.

He'd had to see for himself that she was okay. Honestly, had he expected a broken, sad woman stuck in a dead-end job in the wilds of nowhere?

Yeah, in fact, he had.

When she'd refused to come to Manhattan after her miscarriage, he'd known she was done with him. Though it had smarted, he hadn't been a stranger to rejection from someone he loved. He'd dealt with it and had thrown himself completely into his work, but some perverse part of him had needed, *wanted* to see her again. When he'd left her she'd been so ill, so fragile.

Now she was whole and healthy.

It was like the miscarriage had never happened. She was confident, happy in her job. Hell, she'd even learned how to fly a plane. When he'd seen that jet, he'd been impressed. She wasn't the same girl he'd left behind. It seemed she was stronger for their parting.

Whereas he was not.

He glanced down at his hand and flexed it. The leather of his glove creaked, his hand inside, stiff.

A year ago, he'd been in a car accident during a bad bout of fog on the highway. His hand had been crushed. Quinn flexed his hand again, curling and then releasing it. Yes, it'd been broken and he'd undergone countless surgeries to repair it, but he could still use it. His hand had mended with time. Perhaps Charlotte's heart had, too, in the five years they'd been apart.

He doubted it. When Charlotte had greeted him it'd been so formal. So forced.

"Whoa, that was a bit rough," he remarked, as they hit more disturbance. He was no stranger to flying, but that was the most jarring bit of turbulence he'd ever experienced. Of course, he was used to first-class seats instead of being crammed into a small cockpit beside the pilot, especially an alluring pilot like Charlotte.

His shoulders almost touched hers in the tight space, just a near brush of her body against his sending his blood pumping. Just being in her presence again aroused him. Charlotte was a strong aphrodisiac, like ambrosia, and she had tasted just as sweet, too.

Blast. Get ahold of yourself. You're not some randy med student. You're going to be Chief of Surgery when you return to Toronto.

Only he couldn't get ahold of himself. She looked exactly as she had when he'd first laid eyes on her. The slender figure and bright red curls were exactly the same. Her face, with only the barest hint of makeup, still looked as fresh and innocent. It was like time hadn't touched her.

Perhaps the cold preserves people up here.

Quinn shook his head. He'd never understood her desire to live on top of the world. He hated winter at the best of times. The frigid air seemed to reach down his throat and scald his lungs with ice.

"Is something wrong?" Charlotte asked casually, not looking at him.

"What makes you think something's wrong?"

The plane lurched and she adjusted her controls. "You're muttering to yourself. Not used to a small plane, eh? Prefer first class?"

"Well, at least I can get a drink in first class." He rubbed his hand. "That, and I'm not used to turbulence that seems more like bull-riding at the Calgary Stampede."

Charlotte grinned. "This is mild."

"Good God. Mild? Are you certain?"

She chuckled. He'd always liked her laughter. "Positive. There's a storm coming."

"Did we hit it?"

She shook her head. "Nope. The storm is chasing us. We'll beat it."

Quinn shuddered. *Snow. Ice.* "I don't know how you live up here."

"I like the rugged wilderness."

"I thought you were afraid of bears. Isn't this bear country?"

She laughed, her green eyes twinkling. "This is true."

"You never did tell me why you're afraid of bears."

"It's silly, really."

"Come on, humor me. There's no in-flight movie, either."

"No. I'm not telling you." She grinned and adjusted some more knobs.

"Come on. I promise I won't say anything." He waggled his eyebrows, teasing her.

She shot him a look of disbelief. "No way. And stop that eyebrow-waggling."

"What, this?" He did it again for effect. Quinn had forgotten it drove her batty and he'd forgotten what fun it was to tease her.

"Lord, you look like a demented Groucho Marx or something."

"I'll keep pestering. You know I have a bit of an annoying streak."

"A bit?" A smile quirked her lips. "Fine. It's because I'm afraid of being eaten alive."

He cocked an eyebrow. "Is that so?"

Charlotte's creamy white cheeks stained with crimson and fire flooded his veins as an image of her, naked, flashed through his mind. He could still taste her kisses on his lips, recall her silky hair and her smooth skin under his hands. Their bodies had fit so well together. It had been so right. His body reacted to her presence. So pure and so not the kind of girl his parents would want for him.

They'd never approved of Charlotte but he hadn't cared. He'd pursued her at first because she was good looking, bright and he'd known it would irk his parents to no end. She had not been like the boring girls they'd kept throwing in his path. Charlotte had not been suitable.

No, Charlotte had been exciting and taboo. Somewhere along the way he'd fallen in love with her. Only they'd wanted different things. She'd wanted a family. He hadn't. With his loveless childhood, Quinn knew he wasn't father material.

When his relationship with Charlotte had ended, his mother had reminded him frequently that Charlotte hadn't been the woman for him. His mother did like to rub salt into a wound.

And they'd been right. Charlotte hadn't been the woman for him.

They were so different, but her difference was what had excited him most.

Quinn pushed aside all those thoughts. They would do nothing but get him into trouble. He was a professional.

A surgeon.

The plane jolted and she was thrown against the dash. Quinn unbuckled and reached out, steadying her. The scent of her coconut shampoo wrapped around him, reminding him of the summer they'd spent in Yellowknife, in a cabin on the shores of Great Slave Lake. Endless nights of blistering passion under the midnight sun.

"Are you okay?" he asked, closing the small gap between them. He could see her pulse racing at the base of her throat.

"I'm fine. Fine." She cleared her throat and shrugged her shoulders. Only he didn't move his hands from her shoulders. He enjoyed holding her again and she didn't shrug out of his arms or move from his touch.

"Are you certain?" he asked again. The blush still stained her skin, her gaze locked with his and her breathing quickened. She parted her lips and he fought the urge to steal a kiss from her. But he wanted to.

So badly.

CHAPTER TWO

LET GO OF HER. She didn't want you.

"Charlotte?" His voice cracked, he cleared his throat. "Are you okay?"

She broke the connection and turned away. "I'm fine. You'd better buckle up in case we hit some more turbulence." She didn't look at him but she appeared perturbed.

"Sure." He could take a hint. Quinn cursed himself inwardly for letting his guard down. When he'd decided to come up here he'd told himself to keep emotionally detached from her, but two hours in her presence and he was being swayed by her again. Just being around her and he forgot what had passed between them—for him it was like they'd never been apart.

She was like a drug that intoxicated him quickly.

Charlotte's cold brush-off brought him out of the past into the present, and keenly reminded him of how lonely his life had been without her. He didn't like to be reminded of that.

He buckled back up and looked out the window as the clouds dissipated. In the distance the white landscape became dotted with brightly colored buildings, which appeared to be raised on stilts above the snow, smoke rising steadily from the chimneys.

So this is Cape Recluse.

The cape was at the mercy of the elements and the Northwest Passage surrounded it on three sides. The town itself was nestled against a panorama of majestic mountains. Squinting, he faintly made out what looked like a tiny airstrip on a sheet of ice.

The whole town looked barren and very, very rustic. It was like something out of the old frontier towns of the Wild West, only snow covered. Quinn knew he was on the edge of civilization, here.

This was what Charlotte preferred over New York?

She flicked on the radio and gave out her call number. "Preparing to land."

"Roger that," came the crackling acknowledgment over the line.

Charlotte brought her plane in to land. Quinn was impressed with her piloting abilities as she brought the aircraft to a smooth landing on the slick airstrip. When the wheels of the plane touched the ice, the jet skittered slightly, but Charlotte kept control and then visibly relaxed.

As she swung the plane round towards the small hangar, Quinn saw a group of villagers milling about.

"That's quite a homecoming."

"Yes, well, there's not much winter entertainment up here," Charlotte said.

"I'll bet there isn't." Quinn regretted his muttered comment the moment it had slipped past his lips.

Smooth move.

Charlotte's eyes narrowed and flashed in annoyance, but all she said was, "Well, we'll get you settled."

She taxied the plane into the hangar.

"Sounds good." He could do with a long, hot shower and some sleep, but judging from the size of the town he didn't see any four-star accommodation nearby. The sooner he dealt with Mentlana Tikivik's case, the sooner he could get back to Toronto, and sanity.

* * *

Charlotte's pulse rate felt like a jackhammer at the moment and she hoped Quinn hadn't noticed how much he had affected her.

Damn.

One stupid little embrace during turbulence had set off all sorts of crazy hormones zinging through her body.

His stay in Cape Recluse was going to be more trying than she'd originally thought and had tried to tell herself it would be. To make matters worse, there were no hotels in town and Quinn would be staying with her. He *had* to stay with her.

When his arms had wrapped around her in the cockpit, her blood had ignited and her common sense had wrestled with the side of her that had wanted to toss aside the plane's controls and throw herself into his arms.

Totally irrational.

She was the fly to his spider, apparently.

It wasn't like she was desperate. She'd gone on other dates with good-looking, exciting men, but she hadn't lost her head around them.

And that was the point. Quinn always made her feel giddy, like a lovestruck fool. He was exciting, sexy and handsome, and made her body burn with a pleasure she hadn't felt since he'd left.

Every day she'd be forced to face Quinn, the man who had broken her heart, but she had to do this for Mentlana. She knew she'd be putting her heart at risk, and it had only recently mended since he'd left her for the greener pastures of New York. She'd rarely thought of him for the last couple years.

Liar.

Of course she'd thought about him, even though for the last couple years it hadn't been as constant as it had been before that. Except for one day. Every year on the anniversary of the day she'd miscarried the baby and had nearly bled out, she'd thought of him and what could've been had he not walked away.

Only, what could've been was just a fantasy. Quinn wouldn't have settled down. She realized that now.

Her throat constricted as she tried to swallow down those emotions. When she thought of what could have been, when she thought about the family she'd always dreamed of, she fought the urge to break down in tears.

Don't think about it.

Charlotte took a deep, calming breath, removed her headpiece and climbed out of the cockpit.

"Doc Charley!"

Charlotte glanced up to see George, her paramedic, approaching the plane. She embraced George, who was like a brother to her.

"Good to see you, Doc. Good flight?" he asked, though Charlotte knew he wasn't really *that* concerned about her flight. He was a pilot, too, and the Citation was like his baby. George moved away and stroked the side of the jet for good measure. "Any problems?"

"None. Your baby is fine and the flight was good." She glanced back to see if Quinn was disembarking okay. He appeared to be, as he climbed stiffly out of the cockpit.

"Dr. Devlyn." Charlotte waved him over, and Quinn strode over, his gaze intently focused on George. He didn't respond. Charlotte gritted her teeth. "Quinn, this is George Atavik. He's my paramedic and copilot. George, this is Dr. Devlyn, the specialist from Toronto."

George grinned, flashing brilliant white teeth. His dark eyes lit with sincerity. "Good to meet you, Dr. Devlyn. Thanks for coming up this far north to help out."

"The pleasure is all mine and, please, just call me Quinn," he replied, shaking George's hand. He glanced at her, his dark eyes twinkling mischievously, a look that spoke volumes, like he was undressing her right there on the spot, as he whispered, "Just Quinn."

"George is Mentlana Tikivik's brother," Charlotte said, clearing her throat. Why she'd blurted that information out she didn't know. It was like she wanted Quinn to know there was nothing between George and her. She watched for any sign of reaction from Quinn, but there was none. All he did was nod politely.

"I'll take care of the plane, Doc Charley. I checked the weather satellite earlier and I was worried you were going to be delayed by that storm coming in from Labrador." George chatted away, totally unaware of the tension Charlotte keenly felt hovering over them.

"I was, too, for a moment," she answered absently.

"I'll go and collect my bag," Quinn said, walking back toward the plane, where people in the hangar were unloading his suitcase and some supplies Charlotte had brought up. So like him to be haughty.

It's Quinn.

Even though she knew she shouldn't follow him, Charlotte hurried after him.

"Are you still tired from the trip?" she asked.

"A bit," Quinn answered. "Don't you and George have to deal with the plane?"

"George can handle it. He'll yell if I'm needed."

"He seems like a nice fellow, I hope he makes you happy."

Charlotte did a double take. Quinn thought she was with George and, despite the fact they'd once been intimate, was wishing her happiness. So unlike the selfish man he'd been when he was younger.

"Quinn, George is like a brother to me." Again, why was she telling him that? She should've let him think George was her lover, and then she shuddered at the thought. She'd babysat George at one time and he'd been a terror. "Besides, George is too weird, too into his Westerns. I think that if given the chance, he'd trade in his paramedic bag for a saddle and six-shooter." She said the last part loudly.

"Yeah, yeah, laugh it up. Clint Eastwood is da man!" George called back.

A look of pleasure flashed momentarily across his face. "Well, that makes for a good partnership between physician and paramedic."

"Doc Charley!" The frantic call made both Charlotte and Quinn spin around. Charlotte saw Lorna, the village midwife, come running into the hangar.

Charlotte didn't need to be told. Her instinct kicked in and she grabbed her medical bag from the top of the pile of supplies. "What's happened? Is it Mentlana?"

Lorna nodded. "She started bleeding, and I don't know if it's from the fetus, the placenta or something else."

Oh, God, no.

Charlotte remembered the way she herself had almost bled to death when she'd lost her baby. Sweat broke out across her brow. Charlotte glanced at Quinn, who was standing close to her. His lips were pressed together in a firm line and he looked a little pale as he nodded his understanding, obviously ready to follow her lead.

"Where is she?" Charlotte asked.

"The clinic." Lorna was wringing her hands nervously.

"Thanks, Lorna." Charlotte started running, praying she wasn't too late.

"Is everything okay, Charley?" Mentlana's voice was anxious as Charlotte peeled off the rubber gloves and placed them in the toxic medical waste receptacle.

"Your cervix is irritated, that's all." Charlotte had been relieved on her arrival to see the blood loss was minimal, but enough to worry Lorna. Given all the things wrong with Mentlana and her high-risk pregnancy, Lorna had reacted quickly and done the right thing.

"Well, yours would be irritated, too, if you were carrying around an elephant."

Charlotte chuckled. "I'm going to have Dr. Devlyn, the specialist from Toronto, perform an ultrasound to make sure there's nothing wrong with the placenta or the baby. But the heartbeat is strong, and from the internal, the placenta is still in place. If it had been an abruption there would've been a lot more blood."

And death. Charlotte kept that thought to herself. There was no sense in worrying the pregnant woman over nothing.

Mentlana visibly relaxed as she took her feet out of the stirrups and rearranged the sheet over her lower half. Charlotte ran her hands under the tap and scrubbed them thoroughly.

"Do you want me to get Genen? He's probably climbing the walls."

"Let him wait for a moment. I want to talk to you."

Confused, Charlotte pulled her wheeled stool over to her friend's side nonetheless. Mentlana was leaning up on one elbow, a serious look on her face.

Charlotte knew that look all too well. It meant business.

"What's your question?"

"This doctor from Toronto, he's the one, isn't he?" Mentlana asked.

Charlotte's heart skipped a beat. "What do you mean?"

Mentlana's eyes narrowed, glinting as black as coal as she fixed Charlotte with the serious gaze that made Genen and George almost wet their pants. "Don't lie to me, Charley. This is the guy, right? He's the guy who broke your heart and left after you lost the baby. The one you wouldn't bring home to meet us. The one who, if I wasn't pregnant and in need of him, I'd give a stern kick to the crotch."

Charlotte stood. Letting out an exasperated sigh, she scrubbed her hand over her face. "Yes. Dr. Devlyn is the one."

Mentlana reached out and grabbed her hand. "I know how

hard it is for you to trust him, to bring him here, and I know you're doing it for me and the baby. Thank you."

A sob caught in Charlotte's throat but she controlled it. She forced a wobbly smile and smoothed Mentlana's jet-black hair from her forehead. "I would do anything for you, even face the devil himself—or Devlyn, in this case."

"Witty." Lana chuckled. "Now I'm *really* interested in meeting him."

Charlotte rolled her eyes and padded towards the door. "Well, he does have the bedside manner of a bull in a china shop, most days. Stay tight. I'll bring him in to see you in a moment."

"Tight, right." Mentlana snorted as Charlotte shut the door to the exam room. Just as she'd thought, Genen was pacing, and the rest of the family was crowded into the small reception area of her clinic. Genen almost rushed her as she approached.

Charlotte held up her hands. "It's nothing, just an irritated cervix. Mother and baby are fine, but I'll have the specialist do an ultrasound to be absolutely certain."

Relief washed over Genen's face. "Can I see her now, Charley?"

"Sure. But just Genen," she said, as the entire Atavik and Tikivik clan seemed to rise. Scanning the clinic area, she couldn't see Quinn anywhere. Biting her bottom lip, she headed over to George.

"Where's Dr. Devlyn?"

"In your office. I thought he'd be most comfortable there."

The blood drained from Charlotte's face. "My office?" *Oh, God.* She hadn't had a chance to clear away her personal items, including the cherished, faded old sonogram. The ultrasound he hadn't even bothered to attend. The same sonogram he'd just grunted at when she'd shown it to him.

"Don't you want to see? It's amazing!"

"It's not like you haven't seen a sonogram before."

"I know. But, Quinn, it's our baby."

He shrugged. "I have to go, Charlotte. I'm late for my rounds already."

He hadn't wanted to see it then and even though it was childish, she didn't want to share it with him now. Not after five years. He didn't deserve to see it or share in any part of her grief.

CHAPTER THREE

TRYING NOT TO panic, she thanked George and headed towards her office. She raised her hand to knock and then thought better of it. Why should she knock? It was her office and he was the visitor. She walked in. Quinn wasn't behind her desk, but was staring out the window at the snow swirling over the inlet. He turned when she entered, his face unreadable.

"Is Ms. Tikivik stable?" he asked.

"Yes. It was an irritation of the cervix, but I'd like you to do an ultrasound and check the status of the fetus yourself."

"I will." He glanced back out the window. "I have to say I've never seen so many houses tied down to cables and supported on metal beams. It's like they're a bunch of beach houses or something."

Charlotte couldn't help but smile. "The houses are raised because of permafrost. There are no basements in Cape Recluse. The village also has a lot of high winds. We may seem sheltered, with mountains surrounding us, but it's really very windy. We have to tie everything down."

Quinn's eyebrows arched. "I guess. With no trees to form a windbreak."

"Yeah, you could say that."

"It's quite interesting—the landscape, that is."

Now it was Charlotte's turn to be impressed. He'd never been overly interested in anything else before, beyond the next surgery.

Well, he'd been interested in her until she'd got pregnant and decided to become a family physician.

"Yes. It is an interesting vista," she agreed.

Quinn shivered and then nodded. "This is some community. They all seem to care for one another, like family." He shook his head. "It's like the Brady Bunch up here or something."

"That's because they genuinely do care. It's a small place and everyone knows everybody. There are no secrets."

That caught his attention and he shot her a questioning look. "Really? No secrets?"

"Nope. Not a single one." Suddenly she had a bad case of butterflies. She was nervous. Perhaps it was the fact they were in an enclosed room, alone. After her reaction to him earlier, the last place she wanted to be was in a private office with him.

He strode over to her, his eyes soft, with a twinkle of devilment still dancing there. As he reached out and brushed an errant curl from her face, a zip of delight traveled down her spine. His knuckles brushed her cheek, causing her body to waken. One simple touch from him and her body responded as if it had been in a slumber for the last five years.

Maybe it had. No other man had been able to arouse her by a simple touch before. It angered her that Quinn was the only one who could.

"Don't," she whispered, her voice catching in her throat.

"What?"

"Touch me with familiarity."

Quinn moved his hand. "I'm sorry, Charlotte. It's force of habit, even after all this time."

Tears stung her eyes and she cleared her throat before taking a step back. "You shouldn't keep the Tikiviks waiting."

"Do you have some scrubs for me?"

"Of course. See Rosie at Reception and she'll get you fitted." Charlotte tucked her hair behind her ear as he stared at her, the tension in the room almost palpable. Why wasn't he leaving? "Is there anything else?"

Quinn glanced away. "No. I'll go and see Rosie now."

Quinn walked past her and Charlotte watched him go, un-ease and apprehension twisting her stomach. When he left the room she snatched the picture frame off her desk and stared at the sonogram, thinking about the baby she'd lost. He or she would've been five years old, now, and she couldn't help but wonder if the baby would've had the same sandy-brown hair and deep brown eyes as Quinn. Perhaps their baby would've favored her, with red curls and emerald eyes, or been a mix-ture of them both.

Closing her eyes, she pictured a rambunctious boy, like she always did when she thought about her lost baby. He'd have had rosy cheeks, sandy-brown hair and green eyes. She felt the sting of tears and brushed them away quickly.

Why was she letting herself feel this way again?

Why was she letting Quinn Devlyn in again?

Because I never let him go.

Sighing, she opened her filing cabinet and pushed the pic-ture to the back before locking the drawer. She slipped the key into her pocket. It was really a moot point, now. There *was* no baby of theirs, not now and not ever.

Quinn peeled off the clothes he'd been wearing for the last several hours. He was bone weary and absolutely freezing, but this was the moment where he shone, being a surgical god.

His hand trembled slightly and he gripped it.

Just tired, that was all.

Besides, this was nothing big. Just an ultrasound and a con-sult. If this tremor continued he'd remove himself from the case. The patient's life and that of the baby were more impor-tant than proving to the world he was still a viable surgeon.

You can do this.

Quinn pulled on the scrubs. As he splashed some water on his face, his mind wandered to the sonogram he'd spied on Charlotte's desk.

Their baby.

The one they'd lost. It had been the scariest moment of his life. Not even the accident that had damaged his hand had been as terrifying as the moment when they'd lost their baby. Charlotte had bled badly after she'd miscarried. He'd found her collapsed on the floor of their apartment.

"Hold on, honey. Hold on, Charlotte." He reached down and stroked her pale face.

Quinn shuddered, sending the horrific nightmare back to where it had come from. That moment had been far worse than the accident he'd endured alone.

Seeing the sonogram on her desk, in a frame, had only reminded him of the pain when they'd parted. At the time, he hadn't been too keen on the idea of a baby in their lives. How could he be a good, loving father when he had such a role model as his own cold, detached father? A baby was not part of his plans. However, it had hurt him when she'd lost it, to see her in pain. To watch her grieve and know there was nothing he could do about it. It had made him feel powerless.

And he didn't like feeling powerless. Not in the least.

There were times in the neonatal unit, when dealing with babies born prematurely, that his mind wandered to what might've been.

But that was in the past. Their baby hadn't survived. So he'd told himself it wasn't meant to be, and had instead focused on becoming one of the best surgeons in his field, burying his sadness over the loss in his work.

Now he was at the top of his game.

And lonely as hell.

Another reason why he hated these godforsaken outposts of the North. He didn't get Charlotte's fascination with staying up here.

Even though her life had been spared, the North had still cost him Charlotte.

She had refused to leave and go with him to New York.

Had refused to talk to him or even look at him. All she'd done was hand back the ring, along with everything else he'd given her, because in her note she'd stated she wanted no reminders of him.

Why did she still keep the sonogram?

Of course, he had no right to pry. The baby was gone.

He jammed the clothes he'd taken off into a suitcase, stuffing the unwanted emotions to the dark recesses of his mind, as well. He didn't have time to let his personal feelings get in the way. There was a patient waiting, counting on him. He exited the bathroom, pulling his luggage behind him. The hairs on the back of his neck stood on end and he knew instinctively all eyes were glued to him. Turning, he smiled and waved awkwardly. No one returned his greeting.

Good Lord.

He approached Charlotte's nurse, the one who had given him the scrubs. Lavender scrubs, no less. Quinn made a mental note to see if there were any blue or green in stock. He wasn't partial to any shade of purple. Perhaps he was a bit of a pig for thinking this, but he felt a bit emasculated in such a feminine color.

"Sorry, I don't remember your name," he apologized.

"No worries. I'm Rosie, and I can take your luggage for you, Dr. Devlyn."

"Thanks. And the patient?"

"In exam room one."

"Thanks again."

The eyes, he was pretty sure, followed him all the way to the exam-room door. The tension was so thick you could slice it with a knife. Perhaps they were shocked to see a man in lavender.

Quinn knocked on the door and Charlotte answered. A smug smile tugged at the corner of her lips as she looked him up and down.

"I think that's your color," she teased.

"Think again," he snarled.

Charlotte stifled a giggle and stepped to one side. "Come in."

Quinn entered the large exam room, his gaze resting on the Inuk couple in the corner. The woman was exceptionally pretty, with black hair and eyes to match. There was a dimple in her cheek as she grinned up at her husband.

"Mentlana, Genen, this is Dr. Devlyn. He's the specialist I told you both about."

Genen stood and came over to grasp Quinn's bad hand, shaking it firmly. Quinn didn't wince, even though the man had a strong grip.

Quinn approached Mentlana and was surprised by her measured gaze. This woman was picking him apart with her eyes and he felt like a slab of meat.

"A pleasure to meet you, Mrs. Tikivik."

"And you, Dr. Devlyn. Charley wasn't wrong. You *are* cute."

He arched his brows and held back the grin threatening to erupt.

"Ahem." Charlotte cleared her throat from behind him and now it was his turn to stifle a laugh. Craning his neck, he looked back at her. She was conveniently staring at the ceiling, but her blush was evidence of her embarrassment. He liked the way the pink bloomed in her creamy white cheeks.

Focus.

"Well, thank you for the compliment. I'd like to do an ultrasound, now, if that's okay?" he asked, steering the subject back to the examination. But he planned to use Mentlana's little disclosure of information to get him a manlier color of scrubs. Right now he had a job to do. Now was not the time for frivolity or personal feelings. "Do you have a full bladder?"

"When don't I?" Mentlana replied. "Please, before I burst."

"I'll get the ultrasound machine," Charlotte said.

Charlotte wheeled the machine over and then dimmed the lights, refusing to meet his gaze.

So, I still make her uncomfortable.

That thought secretly pleased him.

Getting to work, he uncovered Mentlana's belly. "Sorry. This is a bit cold."

"That's not cold, Dr. Devlyn. Outside is cold."

He grinned, but didn't engage in any further pleasantries. He had a consult to complete. Quinn placed the probe against her abdomen and began to adjust the dials to get a clearer picture. Genen leaned forward, his eyes transfixed on the image on the monitor.

"Well, from what I can see, your placenta, though previa, is fully attached and not bleeding."

"That's a relief." Genen kissed his wife's hand. "And the baby?"

"The bleeding is not being caused by the baby. I have to run some more tests to determine the severity of the CCAM, but other than that, his heart is beating and he's moving well. His other organs are forming satisfactorily for a gestational age of twenty-one weeks."

"Thank you, Dr. Devlyn. I appreciate it," Mentlana said.

"I want you on bed rest, though." He turned to look at Charlotte. "I'm sure Dr. James will agree with my assessment."

"Yes," Charlotte said. "I think we've had this discussion before."

"For how long?" Mentlana's gaze traveled nervously between him and Charlotte.

"For the remainder of your pregnancy. With your pulmonary embolism and placenta previa alone, it's for the best," Charlotte said, brushing back Mentlana's hair.

Mentlana nodded. "Okay."

"We'll call you when I'm through analyzing your labs and diagnostic images." Quinn wiped the sonogram gel from her abdomen and then turned back to the machine. "Until then, take it easy."

"Sounds good, Doctors."

Quinn saved various shots of the baby's heart and other organs to determine whether or not he would have to do the surgery in utero. It would be better if he could wait until the baby was full term to deliver it via Caesarean and do the operation on the newborn.

He'd done *that* surgery several times since his hand had been damaged.

If the baby could wait until its birth, by then he might be able to figure out a way to get Mentlana to Mount Hope, where his surgical team could assist him. Even Iqaluit would be better than here.

Charlotte may be a competent physician, but she was no surgeon.

She could've been great if she'd only come to New York with me.

Quinn stood up and left. He knew Charlotte followed him, and so did the collective gaze of the mob huddled in the waiting room as they passed to get to Charlotte's office.

Once they were behind the closed doors he wandered over to the window and wrinkled his nose in dissatisfaction at the swirling snowstorm, which had caught up with them.

Then again, it would make a nice photograph and he was glad he'd brought his camera. Since his father's death, he had been indulging in his secret passion for photography. Something his father had always stated was a waste of time.

He was on sabbatical, as his father had just died when Charlotte had called, and he'd planned on taking a trip to India to photograph scenery. Instead, he was up in the High Arctic and not getting paid much to be there.

The money didn't matter to him.

His father would roll over in his grave if he knew, and he already knew how his mother felt about this excursion.

"You don't have time for a charity case, Quinn. You have to prepare to take your father's place!"

God. He hated winter. It probably stemmed from the fact he'd been forced into endless hours of hockey practice by his father, when all Quinn had wanted to do was take photography lessons. Photography hadn't been manly enough for his father, whereas hockey was the sport of champions.

"Don't they have winters in Toronto?" Charlotte asked, breaking the silence.

Quinn glanced back at her. "Pardon?"

"The way you're scowling at the snow."

Quinn shrugged. "You know I hate winter."

"How could I forget?"

"I'm not the only Canadian who does. Think about all the snowbirds that go to warmer climes every winter."

Charlotte's eyes widened. "You want me to picture you as an old man in a RV?" Her eyes twinkled with mischief.

"Ha, ha. Very funny."

"I'm sorry about the scrubs." A devilish smile played across her lips.

"You're not in the least. You enjoyed watching me give the locals a fright."

Charlotte laughed and he couldn't help but join in. "I'll see if George has any spares."

"Much appreciated."

"What do you think of Mentlana's condition?" she asked, mercifully changing the subject.

"Your assessment is correct, though I don't know the severity of the CCAM yet."

"How long will it take you to determine that?" she asked, her voice tight and her lips pursed together in a thin line. He could see she was stressed about Mentlana.

Charlotte always got over-attached to people.

"A few days. I want to be absolutely certain. I sent the scans to your computer and I'll email them to my laptop later. I have an internet stick, because I figured there's no Wi-Fi up here."

Charlotte nodded. "Wise move."

Quinn moved away from the window and took a seat on the opposite side of the desk. As soon as he sat down he noticed the little frame with the sonogram picture was gone. He didn't search the room for it as he didn't want Charlotte to know he'd seen it. Apparently she'd hidden it. It irked him that she was hiding it from him.

Like it had never existed.

Like *they* had never existed. And that saddened him.

He shook that thought away.

"I'm glad it was just an irritated cervix." Charlotte sat across from him, her back ramrod straight, her fingers laced in front of her.

"There are no pools of blood darkening on the scans. The fetus is thriving, despite the CCAM. I take it they knew the gender beforehand. I hope I didn't make a blunder with that."

"They knew."

Quinn nodded. "I'm hoping we can get Mentlana to twenty-five weeks before I even think of doing in utero surgery to repair the lungs—that way, if we have to deliver, the baby has a better chance of survival."

Unlike ours, who miscarried at a mere sixteen weeks.

"In utero surgery is needed?"

"It may not be. We'll monitor her. She may go to term and then the baby's lungs can be repaired after delivery, but if there's much more fluid collection we risk hydrops. If that's the case we'll have to place a shunt in the fetus's lungs so the fluid can drain into the amniotic fluid and take the pressure off the lungs. Then, when the baby is full term, we can resect the lesion on him. Really, that would be the ideal situation."

Quinn rubbed his hand, which had begun to bother him again. He needed to do his strengthening exercises. "There has to be a way to get to Iqaluit, though. You don't have the facilities here to deliver a baby by Caesarean, let alone operate on a fetus in utero."

"She has a pulmonary embolism. I can't fly her."

"What about low altitude?"

"I've thought of it, but with the sudden storms and mountains…it's risky. It would double the flight time."

"It's risky leaving her up here. When the time comes we need to get her to Iqaluit. If she makes it to twenty-four weeks, we need to consider flying her down there."

Charlotte scrubbed her hand over her face. "You're right. I know it. All right, when the time comes we'll fly her at low altitude to Iqaluit, but if her water breaks or a storm hits, we'll have to do it here. I've been stockpiling supplies."

"Supplies won't cut it. I need a *proper* surgical team to assist me. I'm sorry. You alone won't be of any use in this situation."

Charlotte's eyes flashed in annoyance. "I'm more than capable of assisting you, Dr. Devlyn."

"Have you done surgeries here before?" he asked, intrigued.

"Yes, but never this kind. It's why I need you here, Quinn." She reached across the desk and took his hand. Her small, delicate hand fit so snugly in his. Warmth spread across his chest. He wanted to pull her closer to him.

He hadn't realized how much he'd missed her.

Don't. She didn't want you.

Quinn pushed her hand away.

It was too little, too late. There was no going back.

She cleared her throat and her expression was serious. "Will you let me assist, Dr. Devlyn, or do I have to hire help?"

As much as he was tempted to tell her to bring up a surgical team, he knew the money would be coming out of her own pocket and he couldn't do that to her.

"If it comes down to it, I would like you to assist."

CHAPTER FOUR

CHARLOTTE WAS TAKEN aback. She wanted to believe that Quinn trusted her abilities as a surgeon and was willing to let her help save her best friend's baby, but a niggle of self-doubt gnawed at the back of her mind.

She knew what his thoughts about general physicians and surgeons had been in medical school. Quinn had believed in the discipline, drive and focus of training for years in a specialty, which of course had been very egotistical of him. He had been obsessive when it came to his training. In med school he'd do anything to scrub in on any surgery and she knew he never gave up on a challenge. That's why he was at the top of his field so young.

Charlotte hoped he had changed, though she seriously doubted it. As her father had always said, a leopard didn't change its spots.

Why am I worrying about this?

Quinn was no longer her concern. She didn't care what he thought about her chosen career path and, frankly, if he was going to let her assist in a once-in-a-lifetime surgery, she was going to take it.

Even if it was because Quinn had no other option.

"I think I'm going to have a shower and peel myself out of these oh so charming scrubs." Quinn rubbed his hand, wincing momentarily, and then stood up. "Where am I staying and where can I call a cab?"

Guilt assuaged her. She wasn't heartless. He was exhausted and here she was thrusting him straight into the exam room the moment the plane had touched down. Although it hadn't been intentional, it had just happened that way.

"There are no cabs and there's no hotel." Charlotte stood and walked over to the door. She needed an escape route for what she was about to tell him. Even though she hated having to share a clinic space with him for the next twenty-and-some-odd weeks while they monitored Mentlana, it was even worse having to share accommodations with him.

Already it was proving hard to keep her attraction for him under wraps, but there was nothing to be done. Cape Recluse had no hotels, motels or anything of the kind. The people in this town opened up their homes to strangers. Quinn would be more comfortable at her home, which was connected to the clinic, than at the home of someone he didn't know.

"No hotel?" Quinn's eyes widened. "Am I supposed to crash here?" He glanced down at the old brown sofa that had once adorned their college apartment. "I think I'm too old to curl up on the 'Couch of Gibraltar,' here."

"I have a guest bedroom at my place." Heat began to crawl up her neck and she prayed the blush wouldn't reach her face.

"Are you asking me to spend the night?"

"N-no," she stammered.

Quinn grinned and crossed his arms. Even though he thought the lavender emasculated him, that was far from the truth. He was still as sexy as ever and she wanted to tear those scrubs from his body to get to what was underneath.

Whoa, slow down.

Where had that thought come from? True, it'd been a long time since she'd been with a man…the last time having been with Quinn. Her heart skipped a beat just thinking about it. Maybe that was the cure. To have one last night and get him out of her system. Warmth spread through her at the thought of that foolish notion.

Get a grip on yourself.

Sleeping with Quinn Devlyn was the last thing she needed to do.

"So let me get this straight. You're inviting me over to your place to spend the night?" He was teasing. He wasn't going to let it go. Quinn was annoying that way. He moved closer and Charlotte raised her hands and took a step back.

"It's not like it's in my bed. You'll be in the guest bedroom with its *own* bed. Same general house, two separate beds."

Quinn's brown eyes gleamed with devilment. "You're mentioning the word bed quite a lot, whereas I haven't even once."

Charlotte snapped her fingers. "Ha, you just did."

"Someone has bed on the brain," Quinn teased again.

"You're welcome to find your own lodgings, but unless you want to bunk with strangers or build an igloo you're better off staying with me. Trust me, I don't like it, either."

"Igloo? You're pulling my leg."

"No, really, and, trust me, you don't want to. The bears have been bad this year."

"Bears? You mean as in polar bears?" he asked, startled.

"Yes, what other kind of bear do you think I mean? This is the North, my friend." She chuckled at the expression of horror plastered across his face as she left the room. At least it got her out of that conversation with him.

She walked out of her office to retrieve his luggage from Rosie. It was almost time for the clinic to close, but the residents knew she was only next door. She didn't even have to leave the clinic to go home as the door at the far side of the clinic led straight into her humble but comfortable abode.

"I'm here for Dr. Devlyn's luggage."

"Ah." Rosie got up and lifted the luggage, handing it to her. "He packs light."

"Always has."

"I find it strange he didn't bring his own scrubs," Rosie remarked, as she began to collect up her belongings.

Charlotte grinned, thinking about Quinn in his scrubs again. "Do you think we can get some blue or green ones?"

Rosie frowned over the bridge of her rhinestone-studded glasses. "What does he think this is, the local store?"

"I know. But please try for me, Rosie. He's used to the big city where everything is provided to physicians on a silver platter."

"In Canada?" Rosie asked in disbelief.

"Well, no. He had a private practice in New York for a while."

Rosie nodded. "That makes sense. I'll see what I can do." She zipped up her parka. "I'll see you tomorrow, Doc Charley."

"Good night, Rosie."

No sooner had Charlotte uttered the words than the doors of the clinic were flung open. George came rushing in with a stretcher. On it was Wavell Agluclark, a ten-year-old boy who was being taught the ways of his people in traditional hunting. George had his hand clamped over Wavell's thigh, which was bleeding heavily.

Rosie instantly peeled off her parka and quickly went about preparing a room while Charlotte jumped into action.

"What've we got here, George?"

"Deep laceration to the thigh, possibly a nick to the femoral artery," George answered.

"Exam room one is ready for you, Doc Charley," Rosie called out.

"Bring him in." Charlotte began to scrub while Wavell's dad, Sam, and George lifted him from the stretcher onto the exam bed. Wavell's face was pale with blood loss, pain and fear. A twinge of sympathy raced through her. She hated seeing a child in pain, but this wasn't Wavell's first accident. The boy seemed prone to mishaps.

"So what happened this time, Wavell?" she asked, pulling on a pair of rubber gloves, as Wavell was allergic to latex.

"I was cleaning fish after ice fishing, and the knife slipped," he said, through gritted teeth.

"Well, let's take a look."

George removed the gauze he'd been using to compress the wound. Gingerly inspecting the site, Charlotte could tell it was deep, but because the blood was being controlled and not gushing, the femoral artery was probably all right.

Rosie came back into the room.

Charlotte glanced over her shoulder. "I need ten ccs of lidocaine."

"Yes. Right away." Rosie skittered away to the locked medicine cabinet to prepare the local anesthesia.

"I don't like needles," Wavell murmured grumpily.

"I know, buddy, but this needle will numb your wound and I'll be able to stitch it up without you feeling a thing."

"Okay." Wavell pursed his lips. "I can handle it."

Charlotte smiled and ruffled his hair. "You're being very brave." She took the syringe from Rosie and injected around the laceration. "Tell me when you can't feel it and I'll stitch it up."

"Okay." Wavell nodded.

"He's okay, then?" Sam Agluclark asked warily.

"He'll be fine. He didn't cut the artery. Once we sew up his wound he'll need to rest for a couple of days."

"Can't feel it." Wavell slurred slightly.

"Good stuff." Sam was obviously relieved as he looked down at his son.

Rosie handed her a tray with everything she'd need for stitches. Charlotte thoroughly irrigated and cleaned out his cut with saline and Betadine, because she didn't think a knife for gutting fish was exactly clean.

Once she'd thoroughly inspected the site, she began to close the wound with sutures. Wavell didn't make a fuss but held perfectly still as she washed the suture site in more Betadine and packed it with gauze. In fact, Wavell was drifting off from the anesthesia.

"He's all done. I think it's best if you let him have a rest here. I'll get you some painkillers for later. He's to keep his leg elevated and come back in five days to get the sutures removed. No more fishing for a bit. He's lucky it didn't do more damage."

"Thanks, Doc Charley," Sam said.

Charlotte nodded and disposed of the syringes and gloves in the medical waste. Rosie and George cleaned up the rest of the stuff to send for sterilization.

"I'll help you take Wavell home in a couple of hours, Sam," George said. "Why don't you hit the hay, too, Doc Charley? You look beat."

"Thanks, George. I think I will." Charlotte washed up, and then headed back to her office. She was beat. It'd been a long, emotionally draining day. The office was dark and she gently rapped on the door, but there was no answer. Peeking inside, she spied Quinn slumped on the old worn couch. He didn't look comfortable, couldn't be comfortable. She'd crashed on that sofa many a time. And she was a lot smaller than him and even she couldn't fit quite right on it.

The name of the Couch of Gibraltar, as Quinn so lovingly called it, suited it. Although, if her memory served her correctly, she and Quinn had done more than just sleep on that couch when they had been in med school.

Charlotte smiled. He always looked so innocent like this. Too bad his acerbic wit didn't match the angelic impression he gave when he was asleep.

He had been a bit of a wild boy in college. Whereas she'd been quiet and studious, working her way through school on scholarships and odd jobs.

They were such opposites.

What did I ever see in him?

She knew exactly. He was exciting, sexy, thrilling. When he'd first walked into anatomy class with such an air of confidence, it had been like she'd been woken up from a daze. From the moment her dad had died she'd thrown herself into her work, studying, getting the best grades so she could tread in her father's footsteps. She'd ignored guys, had never gone on dates or had a hobby.

Then Quinn Devlyn had waltzed into her life and she'd found herself yearning for more. He had been talented and passionate about his work. Although animal attraction and mind-blowing sex was not what one should base a relationship on. She'd learned that the hard way. Case in point: when she'd needed him most, as she'd lain in that hospital bed after the miscarriage, he hadn't been there in the way she'd needed him to be.

He'd gone to New York to pursue a career in neonatal surgery and she had come here to take over where her father had left off, as a general practitioner in a remote community. What she'd set out to do the moment she'd had to say goodbye to her dad.

Charlotte shook her head, dispelling the painful memory, and then frowned as she looked at Quinn again. This forced cohabitation for the sake of Mentlana was going to test her to the very limits. She tiptoed over to her desk and wrote a note for him, telling him where he could find her. Then she pulled out an afghan and covered him up, but as she bent over to straighten the blanket, which had bunched up on one side, she caught sight of the scars on his right hand.

Surgical scars.

What had happened to him?

From the patterns of the scars it was as though his hand had been broken, severely. He'd had what appeared to be multiple orthopedic surgeries.

The blood drained from her face and she straightened,

backing away from him. What if he couldn't hold a scalpel? That thought was too terrifying.

He can operate. He has to be able to.

If he couldn't, Mentlana's life was at risk. Was he really that arrogant about his surgical abilities?

Yes.

She dismissed the idea. He had to be able to, or he wouldn't have a license and he wouldn't have come. He would've told her the truth.

Really?

Her throat constricted, her stomach knotted with dread. Charlotte backed out of the room and shut the door behind her. She wanted to believe Quinn was still the best fetal surgeon, but her instincts told her he was hiding something, while her heart, her traitorous heart, wanted to give him the benefit of the doubt.

Surgeons have had their hands injured before and had still been able to operate, but for the life of her she couldn't re-call a single name of a surgeon who had done so. Neonatal surgeons needed steady hands for their delicate work. Were Quinn's hands still steady?

Mentlana's baby was like blood to her, and Charlotte couldn't lose another child.

Instead of closing the connecting door between her home and the clinic, she left it slightly ajar, in case Quinn woke up.

Charlotte wandered over to her bookcase, where there was a picture of her father and herself. She took it down and held it, lovingly running her fingers over the glass, as if trying to reach through and touch his face once more.

Dr. Cecil James had been a brilliant surgeon in Toronto. An innovator, a lot like Quinn. But then he'd met a nurse, Amber Lees, who'd had the drive to help others. Her father had given up his practice and headed to the North with Amber, and then they'd had her.

Her father's love of the North, even after the loss of his wife, had been instilled deep into Charlotte's being.

She set the picture back on the shelf and rubbed the ache forming in the back of her neck, trying not to think about the prospect of losing someone else she loved, because if Quinn failed it would be her fault for bringing him up here.

Dammit.

She shouldn't trust him. She couldn't. He'd deceived and hurt her before.

And she wouldn't let him do that to her again.

CHAPTER FIVE

"QUINN."

He woke with a start at the faint whisper of his name. When he prized his eyes open he realized he was in a bed and he hadn't the foggiest idea how he'd ended up there. As he surveyed the room he realized he was in a king-size bed, and the walls were covered in rich cherrywood paneling. Like something found on a fine estate. How had he ended up here? The last thing he recalled was sitting down on the old brown couch in Charlotte's office, waiting for her to come back and take him to her home.

Quinn rubbed his eyes, trying to bring them into focus in the dim light of the room, but everything remained an unfocused haze.

"Quinn." Charlotte seemed to appear from the gloom like an apparition. Quinn gasped at the sight of her, not because she was in his room but because of how she looked. Her red curls tumbled down loose over her creamy shoulders. As he let his gaze rove further down, his breath caught in his throat and his blood ignited into flames. She was wearing a long white silk negligee, slit to the thigh, cut very low and exposing the creamy tops of her breasts.

"Charlotte?" he asked, stupidly because he knew it was her. Who else could it be? He'd seen her in that negligee before, when they'd gone to Niagara Falls. Just thinking of that

night of passion fired his blood, and it seemed like a lifetime ago when he'd experienced such a rush, such a hunger for her.

Quinn shifted and realized he was wearing nothing but a sheet draped across his hips. What'd happened to his clothes?

Who cared?

Had Charlotte undressed him? The thought aroused him. God, he wanted her.

Badly.

"I hope you don't mind," she said, as if reading his mind. She moved closer to the bed but stayed just out of reach. "I took the liberty of undressing you."

Was she crazy?

"No, I don't mind in the least."

A devilish smile crept across her face as she moved to the end of the bed. "I'm so glad you came here, Quinn."

"And I'm glad you asked me."

Quinn got up and moved toward her, closing the distance between them. He took her tiny hand in his. It was so small and delicate. He entwined her slender fingers in his and could feel her pulse racing as he let his thumb stroke her wrist.

"Have you missed me, Quinn?" She bit her bottom lip and then smoothed back the hair from his forehead. "Please, tell me you have." Charlotte pressed her body against his, just a thin piece of fabric separating them.

So close.

Her lips brushed against his throat. Just a simple touch of softness against his neck caused his blood to burn with the fires of a thousand suns. A groan rumbled deep in his chest and he slipped his arms around her waist, holding her close.

"Quinn, have you missed me?" she asked again.

Had he? Or was it just in this moment of lust, his need for her that made him want to drop down on his knees and pour out his heart to her.

Yes. He'd missed her, with every fiber of his being. "Charlotte…" But even in his dreams the words wouldn't come out.

"Kiss me," she whispered, her voice husky with promise. Quinn leaned in.

A draft of cold air startled him awake. Pain traveled up his neck, resulting in a pounding headache at the back of his skull. Quinn glanced down and let out a groan of dismay when he caught sight of lavender.

"God." He scrubbed his hand over his face, stubble scratching his palm. It'd been a dream. The whole thing. Of course it had been a dream. For one thing, he doubted she had a king-size bed and cherrywood paneling in her home. Also, Charlotte wouldn't have come to him, not after what had passed between them five years ago, and this wasn't the first time he'd had this dream, either.

When he first left her he'd dreamt of her over and over again. He'd tried to banish the ghost of her with nameless women, but it hadn't worked. Instead, he'd focused on work. The dreams had faded and hadn't come back so often. In fact, he hadn't had such a vivid fantasy of Charlotte in a long time. He almost wished he hadn't woken up, that he'd been allowed to savor the moment and be with her once more, even if only in a dream, because the love they'd shared once was only that, now.

A dream.

Quinn got up, his body stiff and sore from his sojourn on the sofa. Sleeping on a stone floor would've been preferable to the couch that time had forgotten. His bad hand was numb. He flexed it and the joints cracked. It was his own fault. He'd planned to do his exercises last night but had forgotten.

He shook his hand, trying to get feeling back into it, and then headed out of the office. There was a slightly open door and he headed towards it, following the rich scent of coffee in the air. Quinn paused in the doorway of a small apartment, his breath catching in his throat.

Charlotte was puttering around the kitchen. Her red hair

wasn't loose but was pulled back with an elastic tie. The silky negligee had been replaced with a short, pink cotton nightie covered with garish red hearts. The nightie did have an advantage over the lingerie in his dream, for when she reached up into the cupboard he got a glimpse of her bare, round bottom.

Blood rushed straight from his head to his groin. Charlotte's bottom was like two round, ripe peaches ready for picking. He wanted to squeeze them and knead them with his bare hands.

Calm down.

Only, he couldn't. He remembered the first time he'd seen her, bent over her books, twirling her red curls around her finger and totally engrossed in the text. She'd seemed oblivious to the world around her. The only female who hadn't fawned over him because of his money or his looks. It had intrigued him.

It had been like a game, wooing her. He'd wanted to be the one to capture her, and he had.

As she had captured his heart.

Only he'd never let her know that because he hadn't understood love. How could he, with parents who had shown him not one iota of affection while he'd been growing up?

Charlotte had, though. He missed that.

He leaned against the door, causing it to squeak, and Charlotte whipped around, her cheeks staining with crimson as their gazes locked.

"Quinn, you're...you're up."

"Did you forget about me?"

"No." She glanced down and her face paled. She started yanking on the hem of her nightgown as if trying to make it longer, but to no avail.

Quinn didn't mind in the least.

"I think you did," he teased.

Charlotte rolled her eyes. "Did you spend the whole night on the couch?"

"Yes." He rubbed the crick in his neck. "It's been a long

time since I passed out on that thing. I remember it being a bit more comfortable."

"It was never comfortable. You're just older."

Quinn chuckled and took a seat in one of the mismatched chairs surrounding her retro vinyl kitchen table. She slid a cup of coffee in front of him. "Thanks."

"Are you hungry?"

"Starving." He took a sip of coffee, savoring the warmth spreading down his throat and chipping away at the bitter cold that crept in from outside.

"Why are you shivering?" she asked. "It's not cold in here."

"I can feel the cold seeping in."

Charlotte rolled her eyes again and shook her head. "Pansy. I'm not surprised you're hungry. You didn't eat yesterday."

"Au contraire. I had a delightful five-dollar packet of peanuts on my flight to Iqaluit." His stomach growled. "But I'll take you up on your offer of breakfast."

"Good choice. But first I think I'll change."

"Why? It makes no difference to me."

Charlotte blushed again. "All the same."

Quinn watched her head down the hall, savoring the sight of her thighs. Thighs he wished were parted for him right now. He shifted in his seat, his erection pushing against his scrubs. It was like he was some kind of hard-up adolescent again.

Charlotte returned with her nightgown covered up with a long terrycloth bathrobe. It was a shame. He'd seen her in less, but that short cotton nightie was just as appealing as the silken lingerie of his fantasies. At least the robe was much better than the scrubs he was wearing, which did nothing to hide his arousal.

"Are my bags here?" he asked.

"Just down the hall. The door to the left."

"I think I'll change." He slipped out of the seat as discreetly as he could. His room was easily found and he removed the scrubs, tossing them in the nearby hamper. There was a small basin in the bedroom and he washed his face. He'd shower later, after he'd had something to eat. The scent of bacon drifted down the hall, followed by the familiar sizzle from the stove that made his stomach growl again.

Loudly.

"Just in time." Charlotte grinned as he entered the kitchen and sat back down. She slid bacon and a fried egg onto a plate and set it down in front of him. Quinn couldn't remember the last time he'd had a good home-cooked breakfast like this.

Probably the last time I was with her.

When he'd moved to Manhattan he hadn't cooked at home. Even during the last two years in Toronto he hadn't spent his free time mastering the culinary arts. He'd spent his free time wining and dining, until the accident. After the accident he'd started doing photography, but even then he'd been out taking pictures, not lounging around at home where the hum of silence made him feel utterly alone.

The fork dropped out of his hand and clattered against the plate, his hand frozen and numb. He looked up at Charlotte but her back was turned as she continued frying eggs.

Quinn rubbed his fingers until he could feel them again, wiggling them slowly. He'd just picked up his fork as Charlotte sat down across from him with her plate. He would have to do his exercise later.

After breakfast.

"I could do with a shower," he said, just to break the silence. "That won't be a problem or interrupt your clinic or any appointments, will it?"

She shook her head. "No. Why should it? Anyway, it's Saturday and the clinic is officially closed, so no one should bother you."

Silence descended heavily on Quinn as they ate.

"And what will you do today?" he asked casually, because he had no idea what he was going to do to pass the time. Other than maybe venture out and take some pictures of snow.

"Oh, this and that. I'm always on duty." Charlotte finished eating and took her plate over to the sink.

"Don't you ever get a break?"

"Not really. I'm the only physician around these parts."

"Haven't you ever thought of hiring another doctor?"

Charlotte's brow furrowed in thought. "Yes, and I have tried, believe me. Mostly it's recent grads who come up, but they don't stay long. They stay long enough to get another job."

"Government incentive, then, eh?"

Charlotte nodded. "You've got it. They work the hours required to get med school paid for and then they're off to greener pastures."

"Smart kids."

Charlotte's eyes turned flinty and her spine straightened. "You think so?"

"I do."

"Is that why you came up to Yellowknife with me after residency?"

"Yes." There was no point in hiding the truth from her. His parents hadn't supported him through medical school. Even though he was their only child, they'd still felt he shouldn't have any handouts. When he'd followed Charlotte up to the wilds of the Canadian North it had been for purely selfish reasons and he'd told her why when they'd first got together. Charlotte must've forgotten. However, his presence here this time was because of her.

"I see," she said. Her lips were pressed together in a thin line. He'd seen that look before. She was not pleased with him.

"Look, it's the truth and I'm sorry, but I was always up front about that. Perhaps you forgot?"

"No, you're right. You were up front and you had no qualms about leaving when you were presented with an out."

"You could've come with me," he whispered.

"I didn't want to. I love the North. This was the path I wanted to take."

"I know. I make no apologies for the reasons I came to the North."

"Yes, to flesh out your curriculum vitae. I'm painfully aware of that and don't need the reminder." Charlotte snorted.

"It's a good solid plan and looks great on the résumé."

She shook her head. "Is that the only thing that matters to you?"

"My career, you mean?"

"Of course. What else would I be talking about?" Charlotte set down the dish towel she'd been holding. "I don't want to get into this with you. I already know how you feel about it."

"I'm sorry that my career was important, but it should be the top priority for any physician. Hell, for anyone who busted their ass studying in a tough industry. I'm sorry I thought of my career. Is that what you want to hear? You stayed up here and that was for your career, so why should I feel bad about going after what I wanted?"

He regretted the words the moment they tumbled past his lips. Charlotte bit her lip and shook her head, tossing the dish towel on the counter.

"You're right. You shouldn't. I'm going to go do some paperwork. I've fallen a bit behind. Make yourself at home."

Quinn watched her disappear through her bedroom door. It closed behind her with a thud.

You're an idiot, Devlyn.

He was standing stubborn on the pulpit and ideals he had preached so often. Advice he gave to fledgling surgeons in the field of obstetrics, advice that gave him nothing and no one.

He really did have the personality of a sledgehammer, most days. Pain shot up his arm and he flexed his hand.

Fleshing out his résumé wasn't the only reason he'd come to the North. Charlotte had been the reason. The true reason, and he'd blown it.

He shook the morbid memories away, suddenly craving a

drink. Only he knew Nunavut was a dry territory. Not a drop could be brought in. He'd watched the Mounties confiscate liquor from some guys who had been on their way up for some ice fishing in Iqaluit.

Quinn wandered over to the fridge and opened it. Orange juice beckoned him. He pulled it out and resisted taking a swig straight from the carton. Instead, after opening several cupboards, he found a glass. He poured himself some and drank the tangy juice down in one gulp. It burned his esophagus. Since his accident he was a little bit more sensitive to acidic things, but the burn felt good.

The burn helped him forget.

"You've already made up your mind. You don't need my approval." She was lying in the bed, so pale against the crisp white hospital bedding. The IV was still embedded in her vein, giving a transfusion. She was pallid as she stared at the far wall, not responding to his announcement about going to Manhattan to a lucrative job.

Didn't she understand? Life would be better for both of them.

"Charlotte..."

"No." She turned and looked at him, her face devoid of expression. *"No."*

The sound of shattering glass shook away the ghosts of his past and he stared in disbelief at the shards on her linoleum floor. His bad hand had frozen in a crab-like vise.

Quinn cursed wearily. He cleaned up the shards of glass and then headed over to the computer in the corner and wiggled the mouse. The monitor came on with a faint hum and he went directly to the folder on the desktop. Tikivik, Mentlana. He clicked on the pictures and brought up the multiple sonograms of Mentlana's baby.

Although the baby was thriving, the lesions in the paracheynma were quite visible.

Dammit.

If the lesions continued to grow then fluid would begin to collect in the lungs and he would be forced to perform in utero surgery.

Quinn rubbed his eyes, trying to shake the sleep out of them. He wasn't sure if he was up to this in these conditions, but he'd promised Charlotte. It was the least he could to do make up for the hurt he'd caused her five years ago.

Perhaps I won't have to perform the surgery.

Perhaps he could get Mentlana down to Toronto where he *could* perform the surgery, and if not him, someone just as good as him.

He'd see to it personally.

When Charlotte came out of her bedroom, Quinn was nowhere to be seen and even though she was frustrated with him, she wondered where he'd got to. She snuck off to her office, intending to spend the day doing some administrative stuff.

For an hour Charlotte stared at the paperwork. She'd been holding the same manila folder for what seemed like forever.

"This is ridiculous." She dropped the folder back onto the large amount of files teetering on her desk.

Get a grip.

She'd known when she'd called Quinn up here that it would be hard to deal with him. She'd known that, but she'd been willing to ignore her own hurt feelings, her attraction to him for the sake of Mentlana and her baby.

Why was she mad that he'd followed his dreams, just like she'd chosen to stay in the North?

Because it broke your heart that he left you.

Yet here she was, hiding away in her office instead of doing what she always did on a lazy Saturday morning, which was slumming around her house and enjoying the solitude. But she didn't want to appear like a bum in front of him.

So, what? She shouldn't give two hoots that he was in her

house. She was the reason he'd come up here, so why was she allowing Quinn Devlyn to dictate her schedule?

I'm not going to let him.

Charlotte stood up and marched purposefully, head held high, to her house. She opened the door with a "look at me, here I am" attitude and was stunned that Quinn was nowhere in the vicinity of her living area. His plate was still on the table, her carton of orange juice was sitting on the counter and her computer's tropical-fish screensaver bubbled with activity.

"Quinn?" she called out cautiously, but there was no answer.

Great. She mustered up the courage to face him, to show him that she didn't care he was here. To prove to him that he didn't affect her anymore. And he wasn't even here to see it.

Blast.

Charlotte ran her fingers through her tangle of curls and proceeded into the kitchen.

Just like him, leaving a mess behind.

His residence, before they'd roomed together, had been known as the sty for very good reason. The man was a meticulous surgeon but a veritable pig, though Rosie would say the same about her filing habits.

She picked up the orange-juice carton and shook it slightly. There was a bit of juice in it, but when she peered inside there was barely any worth keeping. Except orange juice was damn expensive up here. She'd treated herself to this carton. Charlotte chugged the remainder of the juice so she wouldn't waste a single drop.

A smile tugged the corners of her lips briefly as she recalled the numerous arguments they'd had over his propensity to leave barely a dribble in the bottom of a carton.

The last time, they'd fought over a carton of eggnog during Christmas and they'd ended up making love under the Christmas tree.

Her pulse raced as that memory replayed in her head like a

cozy movie. It'd been so long since she had thought about it. Her heart began to beat faster and butterflies began to swirl around in her stomach.

Damn.

Charlotte crumpled the carton in her hand before tossing it out under the sink. She slammed the cupboard shut, angry at herself for letting herself *feel* this way about Quinn again.

"Domestic duties prevail over paperwork?"

Charlotte startled and spun around. He was inches from her, half-naked. The scent of his body wash was masculine and spicy as she inhaled deeply.

"Uh—uh," she stuttered, and backed up to the counter. She gripped the cheap melamine as if her life depended on it.

"What?" he asked, cocking an eyebrow. "I thought I'd shower and wash off that certain smell that seems to permeate most planes."

Charlotte couldn't think straight as her gaze trailed hungrily down his body, abruptly ending at the tropical beach towel tied around his waist.

His hair curled and glistened with drops of moisture. She ran her tongue over her lips. Oh, how she wanted to run her tongue over his chest, particularly around his nipples, which she knew were particularly sensitive.

"Charlotte, you're starting to scare me."

She shook her head. "Sorry." She turned back to the sink and turned on the faucet, hoping the rushing water would drown out the erratic beat of her pulse and make him move away. "Yeah, going to do some dishes."

Only he didn't move away. He moved closer, and the heat of his body permeated her back, through the thick sweater and turtleneck she was wearing. Gooseflesh broke across her skin and she held her breath.

"Is there anything I can help you with, Charlotte?" he asked, his breath branding her flesh at the base of her neck.

Charlotte turned around again, staring deep into his deep

brown eyes. *Oh, God.* She was falling again. She had no strength when it came to him. He still made her weak at the knees.

"I…"

"What do you need, Charlotte?" He reached out and ran his knuckles against her cheek. "Tell me what you need. I'd do anything for you. You know that."

CHAPTER SIX

HE WAS SO close to her that her heart was racing. Her traitorous body was reacting to him.

"Charlotte," he whispered, and reached out to touch her.

"Hey, Doc… Whoa…sorry!"

Quinn jumped back and Charlotte saw George, a shocked look on his face, standing dumbstruck between her clinic and her home. In his hand was a plastic bag bulging with what looked like blue-and-green scrubs.

"George, come in. Dr. Devlyn and I were just talking about…" She trailed off, her brain totally blank, and Quinn just cleared his throat. He was absolutely no help.

George blushed and looked away, staring at the ceiling. "Sorry, Doc Charley. I should've knocked."

"No, it's okay, George. I was just doing dishes." She pushed past Quinn, feeling humiliated that George had walked in on them in such a compromising position. George would definitely blab about this to Mentlana and she'd never be able to live it down. Ignoring what had happened, she feigned nonchalance. "Is something wrong, George?"

"Nothing. I just brought some scrubs and came to remind you about a certain appointment today." He pointed at his watch. "You didn't forget, right?"

"Shoot," she cursed. She had. Today was her scheduled checkup on Anernerk Kamuk, Cape Recluse's oldest woman and George's grandmother. The woman who had taken in Charlotte when her father had died. Anernerk would certainly have something to say if she was late for the checkup. "I'll be ready in a few, George."

George nodded, a funny smile plastered across his face. "Okay, Doc Charley." His dark gaze landed on Quinn. "Dr. Devlyn, pleasure to see you again."

Charlotte could hear his chuckles as he closed the door to her clinic.

Dammit.

"What did you forget?" Quinn asked.

"Today is my bi-weekly check on Cape Recluse's oldest resident. She's one hundred and one, and an artist."

Quinn's eyes flew open in surprise. "One hundred and one?"

"Hard of hearing, Devlyn?" She grabbed her parka off the coat rack, but a smile tweaked at the corners of her lips.

"I'm sorry. I'm amazed, frankly. In my line of work I don't meet many people who've passed the century mark."

"It's the fresh air up here." She fished around in her pocket for the keys to her snowmobile.

"You said she's an artist. Would I know her work?" Quinn asked.

"Doubtful. Unless you're an expert in traditional Inukti-tut artwork."

"Ah, no." Quinn rubbed the back of his neck. "Don't get me wrong, though. I've seen some really intriguing native art in New York."

"Her name is Anernerk Kamuk. Does that name ring a bell in the 'it' crowd of Manhattan?"

"Not in the art scene, no, but didn't you live with her after your father died?"

Charlotte was impressed. "Oh, so you actually did listen to me when I spoke."

Quinn rolled his eyes. "Give me some credit."

Charlotte blushed. "Sorry. Yes. She's George and Mentlana's grandmother and she took me in when my dad died. Look, I have to get going or she'll raise a stink."

"Can I come?"

Charlotte paused in the middle of rummaging through her bag and stared at Quinn. "You...you want to come?"

Quinn ran a hand through his damp hair. "Yeah. If that's okay?"

She blinked in disbelief. "Sure. Can you be ready in ten minutes? I have to collect a few things from the clinic. Dress warmly and I'll meet you outside."

"Excellent. See you in ten."

Charlotte watched him pad off towards her guest bedroom. When the door shut she shook herself out of her daze and headed into her clinic to collect her bag and instruments. Actually, she was quite looking forward to seeing how Quinn dealt with Anernerk. He'd never had the best people skills when dealing with non-medical professionals, and Anernerk was a bit of a handful at the best of times.

She was going to eat Quinn alive and that thought gave Charlotte a secret thrill. It would be an entertaining appointment, that was for sure.

As she shoved Anernerk's file in her rucksack, Quinn entered her office. He was, surprisingly, kitted out in appropriate cold-weather gear and she was impressed he'd done his homework before coming up here.

"Ready?" she asked with a bit of trepidation.

"Whenever you are."

Charlotte nodded and led him outside. George was waiting on his snowmobile, ready to lead the way through the snowdrifts to the cabin on the outskirts of Cape Recluse, where Anernerk lived and still worked as an important Inuk artist.

"Hey, Dr. Devlyn. Good to see you're going with us. Grandma sure likes to get her hands on fresh meat." George chuckled again and, despite the bitter cold, Charlotte felt her face heat with a blush.

She sent a silent warning of *shut up* to George as she pulled her rucksack on. Charlotte mounted her snowmobile and glanced over her shoulder at Quinn, who was still standing by the door, shifting from foot to foot.

"Nervous?" she asked, pointedly staring at his shuffling feet.

"No. I'm freezing out here. I'm trying to keep the circulation going in my lower extremities."

Charlotte bit back her smile. "Well, let's get going. It's freaking cold out here."

Quinn chuckled and climbed on behind her. His body nestled against her back, his arms wrapped around her waist. Even though many layers of thick clothing and snowsuits separated them, she squirmed in her seat. She was suddenly very warm and it wasn't her winter clothing that was causing it.

"Are you sure you're not nervous, Devlyn?" she teased, trying to dispel her own nervousness at having him so close to her.

"Not in the least," he said. Although something in his voice told her she wasn't the only one feeling a bit edgy about being so close together again. She smiled and revved the engine. It felt so good to have his arms wrapped around her.

"Hold on to your hat."

"Wagons, ho," George shouted above the roar of the Bombardier machines, pumping his fist into the air. They took off across the snow, northeast toward the sea and Anernerk's home.

Charlotte had tried time and time again to get Anernerk to move closer to the clinic, into the main town with one of her children. Anernerk refused on the grounds that the spirits had told her that in order to paint, she needed to see where the sea met the sky without the clutter of town in the way.

A thin column of smoke rose in the air as they crested a

bank of snow. Charlotte let out an inward sigh of relief, glad to know Anernerk was still alive. Anernerk also refused most modern technologies and didn't have a phone.

Anernerk's little red house on high stilts looked warm and inviting. This was where Charlotte had lived when her father had died. This was home. Charlotte parked her snowmobile beside George's. George was humming and grinned at Quinn as he stumbled off the back of her snowmobile.

"Your first time, Dr. Devlyn?"

"On a snowmobile? Yes." Quinn chuckled. "I guess you could say I am a virgin in that respect."

George let out a large guffaw. "Well, you're a virgin no more, Dr. Devlyn. You're officially deflowered."

Charlotte rolled her eyes at the men's childish banter. The door to Anernerk's door swung open quickly to reveal a little wrinkled face peering outside. Dark eyes flashed under a mass of wrinkles.

"Are you just going to stand out there all day? I'm not going getting any younger, you know," she called down from her porch high above them.

"Oh, hush, Anernerk. We're coming, we're coming."

Quinn was stunned by the Inuk woman. Though she was a mass of wrinkles and weathered skin, he wouldn't have guessed from her fluid movements that she was over a century.

Anernerk's beetle-black gaze rested on him. There was a twinkle to them and a smile tugged at the corners of her lips. The intensity of her perusal unnerved Quinn slightly. It was as if the old woman was peering deep into his soul.

"Who've you brought to visit, Doc Charley?" Anernerk asked.

"A friend of mine from med school. He's come here to take care of Mentlana."

The woman's eyes widened. "Mentlana? Well, this is good

news indeed." Anernerk stepped aside as George and Charlotte crossed the threshold into her home.

Quinn followed up the steps, seeking the warmth that emanated from the wood stove in the center of the large room of Anernerk's clapboard shanty, which, like most of the other homes, was tethered down and on stilts. He peeled off his coat and hung it on a peg near the wood stove.

He rubbed his hands together, fast. Even though he had been wearing thick mittens, which the man at the wilderness store had assured him would keep out the cold, the bitter temperature of the top of the world still clung to his skin, sending its frosty tendrils deep into his body. His hands ached and he couldn't get the feeling back into them, no matter how hard he rubbed.

The hairs on the back of his neck stood on end and he had the sense that someone was staring at him. Quinn craned his neck and caught Anernerk's gaze. She was watching him, a strange look on her face. His face heated and he slid his hands into his pockets.

"Anernerk, how are you feeling today?" Charlotte asked.

Anernerk snorted. "How do you think I feel, Doc Charley? Cranky. I'm cranky today."

George, who Quinn had lost sight of, came in through another door on the far side of the room with a load of firewood in his arms.

"She's always cranky, Doc. You should know that by now."

Charlotte smiled patiently as she rolled up the woman's sleeve and pulled out a blood-pressure monitor. The rip of Velcro echoed in Anernerk's sparse cabin, but it was then that Quinn glanced at the walls and realized what he was actually looking at.

"Oh, my God," he whispered.

He moved closer to the nearest wall, enraptured by the thick, bold lines and swirl of primeval colors.

"Pretty cool, eh, Doc Dev?" George said.

"It's...it's like nothing I've ever seen."

Anernerk chuckled over the top of the steady pumping of the blood-pressure cuff. "I think your friend fancies my art, Charlotte."

Quinn spun round. "You've done all of this? This is your art?"

Anernerk nodded slowly, grinning, obviously pleased with his awe. "I was taught by my grandfather. A shaman. Way back when Nunavut was just a lowly outpost on the far reaches of the Northwest Territories and Iqaluit was known as Frobisher Bay."

"I've seen some of these in The Met."

Charlotte grinned. "Yes, Anernerk's art is world renowned. I told you she was an artist."

"Yes, but I had no idea she was this prolific. I can't believe I'm standing here in front of the originals."

"Of course." Anernerk rubbed her hand as Charlotte removed the cuff. "Not so hard next time, Charlotte. There's no meat left on these bones."

"Hush," Charlotte chastised gently.

Quinn found himself drawn immediately to one particular painting, one that featured a man and a woman. The man was harpooning a walrus and the woman was sewing and casting the man evil looks. He felt a bit dizzy and sick staring at it and he didn't know why.

"Hold tight, Anernerk. I have to sterilize this," Quinn heard Charlotte say, and he glanced at her briefly to see her head towards the kitchen, which was tucked off in the corner behind some swing doors.

Quinn tore his gaze away and came face-to-face with Anernerk. She was staring at him.

"I see you're particularly drawn to the depiction of the obstinate man. Do you know the story?"

"No, I don't."

"Come sit by the fire, Dr. Devlyn. I have some liniment for your hands."

"What are you talking about?"

"You may be able to fool other people with your walls, Dr. Devlyn, but you don't fool me."

"I don't?"

Anernerk shook her head. "Come, and I'll tell you all about the obstinate man."

Quinn didn't move and Anernerk rolled her eyes.

"Dr. Devlyn, I may be older than time itself but I don't bite…much." She grinned, displaying her missing teeth. She looked like those typical old witches he used to be terrified of as a child, but there was no malice about Anernerk Kamuk. He nodded and allowed her to lead him to two rockers that sat near the wood stove.

Quinn sat across from her.

"I think this tale will hit you personally, Dr. Devlyn. I think you'll find similarities between your destiny and the destiny of my dear Charlotte." Anernerk reached down in a big basket, which was overflowing with various yarns and knitting needles. She pulled out a dark innocuous bottle with no label.

"How do you know about me and Charlotte?" Quinn asked, intrigued.

Anernerk's black eyes twinkled. "There are no secrets in Cape Recluse, Dr. Devlyn."

"Are you some kind of mind-reader or shaman yourself, Anernerk?"

She raised a thick gray eyebrow. "Are you crazy? Of course not. Just because I'm Inuk doesn't mean I can converse with Nanook of the North or anything." She laughed. "Besides, I talk to Mentlana."

"Mentlana is on bed rest. She's not supposed to leave Cape Recluse. Is she coming out here, Anernerk? I need to know."

"No, of course not!" Anernerk chuckled conspiratorially and pulled out a small phone from her trouser pocket. "Shh.

Don't tell. It'll ruin the whole illusion for George and Charlotte." She hid the phone back in her pocket. "Besides, I like their visits."

Quinn couldn't help but laugh. "You have a smartphone?"

"How else do I keep in touch with my agent? The laptop is in my underwear drawer. Ain't nobody going in there. Now, where was I?"

"You were going to tell me about the obstinate man and the significance it plays in respect to me and Charlotte."

"Give me your hands," Anernerk ordered.

Quinn held them out. Her hands were rough but strong. She undid the bottle and poured the thick corn-syrupy-looking liquid into his hand. It instantly warmed as it touched him. Anernerk began to rub his shattered hand vigorously and the aches and pains began to fade as the old woman's liniment began to work some kind of magic on him. It was better than the exercise regime his physiotherapist forced on him.

"There once was a very stubborn man. Not unlike yourself, Dr. Devlyn. His wife lost their child, but instead of letting her mourn he made her work for him. As she worked, the Moon Man's dog came out and attacked this obstinate man for making his wife work before her mourning time was done.

"The man overcame the dog, killing him. The Moon Man came and fought the obstinate man, but again he was no match for such stubbornness. The obstinate man won. The Moon Man invited him to join him at his home, but told him to take the dark side of the rock and not come around the easier sunny side, or he would lose his heart."

"Lose his heart?"

Anernerk smiled and continued rubbing his hand. "The easiest path is not always the wisest, Dr. Devlyn."

"Is that so?" Quinn wanted to change the subject, but he had the feeling he wouldn't be able to.

"So the obstinate man came around the sunny side and saw an old woman sitting there, sharpening a blade. He thought he could overcome the old woman. She was weak and feeble, whereas he was strong, but he overestimated his ability and lost consciousness. When he came to, his heart had been torn from him.

"The Moon Man saved him, returning to him his broken, tattered heart. It was then that the stubborn man saw the evil, dark thoughts coming from his wife and what he had done to her, how he had hurt her by forcing her to work before her mourning time was done."

Quinn's throat constricted and he glanced towards the kitchen. He could hear water boiling and in his mind's eye he could envision Charlotte cleaning the instruments thoroughly. Did she have dark thoughts about him?

He was pretty certain she did.

"No. You're being stubborn, Quinn. Why do I have to give up my life here?"

"What kind of life is this?"

"A good life."

"We can have a good life in Manhattan."

Tears ran down her face and she turned her head away. *"No."*

"How do your hands feel now, Dr. Devlyn?"

Quinn shook himself out of his stupor and flexed his hands. They were warm, pliable.

"Ahem."

He looked up to see Charlotte leaning against a post, expressions of confusion and intrigue playing across her face.

"Thank you, Mrs. Kamuk."

He stood up and jammed his hands quickly in his pockets.

Anernerk chuckled and then whispered under her breath, "Stubborn, Dr. Devlyn. So stubborn." She looked back at Charlotte. "So, are you ready for your quart of blood, Doc Charlotte?"

Charlotte *tsked* and Quinn moved away so Charlotte could do her work. Quinn watched in admiration. She was so sure of herself now, and though he hadn't seen it at the time, this had been the right path for her.

The path away from him.

CHAPTER SEVEN

CHARLOTTE WAS CLEANING up the rest of her instruments and tucking away the specimens from Anernerk. The resident old coot was back in her rocking chair, knitting and telling stories as her needles clicked together. George was sitting beside her, listening to her and laughing.

Sometimes Charlotte wondered if it was George, the overly concerned grandson, who insisted on these visits out here. Everyone in Cape Recluse loved Anernerk.

Charlotte smiled as she watched the woman who had raised her for over a decade, warmth flooding her veins as she recalled all the good times she and Anernerk had shared. How Anernerk's entire family had welcomed her.

When her father had died she'd had no one. Her father had had no other family except distant cousins. It'd been the same on her mother's side. Charlotte often wondered if it was why her parents had been drawn to each other. Her parents had both been orphans.

As their daughter had become.

The only difference was that Charlotte had had people to love and take care of her. Her parents hadn't had someone like Anernerk to take them in.

She felt blessed.

Anernerk was as healthy as could be for someone over a century old. There was nothing to worry about in regard to the old woman's physical well-being. Charlotte was more worried about what she'd seen between Anernerk and Quinn. Anernerk had a way with people. She could win them over, charm them, and they ate up everything she said.

Even Quinn, who had never believed in all these old hokey remedies and anything even mildly spiritual in nature, especially when it came to medicine, had been mesmerized.

Charlotte had watched Anernerk rub his hands and she had also seen how quickly Quinn had hidden them and brushed off Anernerk when he'd realized she was standing there.

Why was he hiding it from her? What had happened to him?

It wasn't rocket science for Charlotte to figure out in ten seconds that he'd been injured, but he didn't seem bothered by it. Still, she needed to have a frank talk with him about the surgery.

Mentlana was not going to be used as a guinea pig to see if Quinn Devlyn's masterful surgical skills were still intact. There was a reason people donated their bodies to science.

Hell, there were dummies now that could be used to mimic surgery. He could practice on one of them, but not Mentlana.

Charlotte snapped her bag shut and wandered over to him. He was still standing in front of Anernerk's paintings. Staring at them in awe.

"I didn't think you were so interested in Inuktitut art, Quinn."

"I wasn't until I saw an auction at Christie's in Manhattan about four years ago. It was to raise money for a charity and Anernerk Kamuk's art was prominently featured. I didn't recognize the name when you said it. They raised over a million dollars that night and Anernerk's lithograph of Kagssagussuk accounted for a quarter of that million."

"Ah, so you became interested in it because of its worth."

Quinn looked at her, his gaze so intent it sent a shiver of delight down her back. He leaned in closer and she closed her eyes, reveling in the feel of his hot breath against her neck. "It was a beautiful piece. I was ignorant and had no idea."

Charlotte shrugged. "I'm impressed. But you don't know the stories related to them."

Quinn chuckled and moved away. "No, those I didn't know. That information is not readily available in Manhattan and I didn't have the time to really go searching. My practice was flourishing by then." His self-satisfied grin made her grind her teeth just a little.

She spun round. "Well, George, I think we've outstayed our welcome."

"You going?" Anernerk put down her knitting. "You just got here."

Charlotte grinned at her elderly patient. "Anernerk, we got here three hours ago."

Anernerk stood up. "I'll make you something to eat." She turned round and fixed her impenetrable gaze on Quinn. "How about muktuk, Dr. Devlyn? I can make you a nice meal of muktuk."

Quinn's eyes widened and he looked at Charlotte. Even though she was tempted to let him eat some blubber, which was what muktuk was, she wasn't that heartless. Charlotte shook her head subtly.

"Ah, thank you, Mrs. Kamuk, but I think just this time I am going to forgo your delicacy of muktuk," Quinn replied with grace.

Anernerk's eyes narrowed as she stared at Charlotte, then she crossed her arms and snorted. "All right. But at least it puts meat on your bones. Dr. Devlyn is too skinny for my liking."

"Hah!" George chuckled, jamming on his cap. "Meat on your bones, eh, Aanak? Hasn't seemed to do you any good."

Anernerk directed her wrath at George by slapping him across the back of the head.

"I thought her name was Anernerk?" Quinn whispered out of the side of his mouth.

"Aanak is the Inuk word for grandmother," Charlotte explained.

"Ah." Quinn nodded.

Charlotte stifled another laugh and Quinn looked a bit awestruck by it all. Then again, he didn't really have much interaction with others. Even when they had been together she wasn't absolutely sure if Quinn had had any *real* friends.

When they had been in medical school and interning, his whole life had been the hospital, and she'd never met his family. In fact, for a long time she hadn't thought he had any family as he rarely mentioned them. Then one day, after they had settled in Yellowknife, he'd shown up with two air tickets for Toronto. She had been going to fly out to Toronto to meet his mother and father, but two weeks before the flight she'd miscarried.

His father died. Was his mother still alive?

It made her pity him. She had lost the only parent she had known before she'd gone into med school, but she'd had the Tikiviks, she'd had Mentlana, she'd had a home.

Cape Recluse.

She had lived here for ten years before med school. It was why she'd wanted to become a physician and work in the northern communities. If her father had had access to a physician, he might not have died from the aneurysm that had claimed his life.

"Sorry, Aanak," George grumbled, rubbing the back of his head where Anernerk had cuffed him. He bent down and laid a kiss on Anernerk's cheek. Although Anernerk still looked a bit put out, Charlotte could tell she was mollified by George's apology. George snuck out the front door into the cold.

"It was a pleasure to meet you, Mrs. Kamuk."

"And you, Dr. Devlyn. I do hope I get to see you again before you leave us."

Quinn grinned and followed George outside. Anernerk turned her focused black gaze on Charlotte.

"I'll come out and see you again soon, Anernerk." Charlotte embraced the old woman.

"Find it somewhere in your heart to forgive him, Charlotte." Anernerk tucked Charlotte's red curls behind her ear. "He's a good man, just obstinate."

Charlotte's throat tightened and she fought back the tears that threatened to spill. "I'll see you in a couple of weeks."

Anernerk nodded. "You take my advice." She held out a bottle. Charlotte looked at the brown bottle in confusion. "Give it to Dr. Devlyn. He needs it. It will help him heal on the outside, anyway."

Charlotte nodded and stuffed the bottle in her pocket. "See you later."

Anernerk nodded, her eyes glistening as she hugged Charlotte tightly again.

George and Quinn were waiting for her, George on his snowmobile and Quinn shuffling back and forth in the cold, waiting for her.

She made sure her backpack was secure and climbed onto her snowmobile.

Anernerk poked her head out the door. "Next time you come I'm making Dr. Devlyn a nice big meal of muktuk, and there will be no refusal."

Quinn waved and Anernerk shut the door. "What the hell is muktuk?"

"Blubber," Charlotte replied, as she slid on her goggles. She glanced over her shoulder and saw Quinn's eyes widen.

"You're joking…right?"

Charlotte chuckled. "Nope."

"Good God!" Quinn made a choking sound, like he was going to retch.

George, sitting on the snowmobile beside them, grinned. "Aw, c'mon, Dr. Dev. It's not as bad as some of that stuff you hoity-toity physicians eat down there in Manhattan."

"Like what?" Quinn asked.

"Foie gras, caviar, tentacles." George made a wiggly motion with his hand and stuck out his tongue. "Gross."

Quinn laughed. "I'll have you know—"

"Enough!" Charlotte interrupted. "If you two have forgotten, it's below freezing out here. You can talk about strange gastronomical treats at the clinic, in the warmth. Right now, I'd really like to head back to Cape Recluse before the lab samples freeze." She turned and glared at George. "And if they do freeze, guess who's coming back to take them again?"

"Right you are, Doc Charley." George revved his snowmobile. "Let's go." He shot off west back towards town and Charlotte followed, trying to ignore Quinn's arms around her, his body pressed against her as she raced to get back to the warmth of her home and clinic.

Honestly. Men.

Quinn did take his debate about cuisine inside with George. He quite liked George, which was odd. Especially as he'd considered George competition when he'd first arrived, but Charlotte had quickly quelled any thoughts on that score. Now, George was like a buddy. Quinn knew he didn't make friends easily and didn't have many people he really considered friends. His parents hadn't encouraged any camaraderie in his childhood. Only competition.

The only real friend he'd made had been Charlotte, and look how that had turned out. He'd hurt her. Terribly.

The hum of the centrifuge echoed in the quiet clinic and he followed the noise to her little lab at the far corner of the building.

He paused in the doorway; she was hunched over the counter, her head down on her arms, watching the whirling of the machine.

He wished he had his camera on hand so he could capture this moment. She was so beautiful. Her red curls were tied back, except for one errant strand, which every so often she would blow out of her face. Quinn could remember lying in bed with her on their days off, when they'd had hours and no one to disturb them, and he would take that one curl and wrap it around his finger, as she had done that first time he'd seen her. It had been so soft and he'd felt so relaxed, so at home with her.

He'd never felt that way before meeting her.

His father had been a workaholic and the best damn cardio-thoracic surgeon in Toronto. It was ironic it had been a myocardial infarction that had killed him. Quinn's mother had set her son on a pedestal when he'd got into medical school at Harvard. She'd expected the same results as his father had achieved in his chosen field, not ever accepting any failure from him.

Quinn remembered how angry his mother had been when he had started dating Charlotte.

It had made him wonder, later, when he'd realized how foolish he had been to lose Charlotte, if his parents had ever truly loved each other.

Quinn hadn't realized it at the time, but Charlotte had made life worth living and he'd thrown it all away.

As if sensing his presence, she turned her head, her eyes widening when she saw him. She sat up and tucked the lock of hair behind her ear.

"Is something wrong, Quinn?"

"No… Yes."

"Is it something I can help you with?" There was a look of anticipation on her face, and she bit her lip, almost as if she was silently urging him to talk.

He clenched his fist, biting back the pain.

No.

"Just wanted to know what you wanted for dinner."

Charlotte chuckled. "Since when do you cook? Never, if I recall."

Quinn laughed and glanced down at the pristine tiled

floor. "I don't suppose there is any takeout in Cape Recluse, is there?"

Charlotte shook her head. "No takeout, but there is a diner. Would you like to go get some there?"

"As long as I'm not forced to eat that blubber stuff, sure."

Charlotte smiled, her grin lighting up the dimness of the lab. "Let me just put Anernerk's specimens away and we can grab something to eat."

Quinn tracked her movements. God, she was beautiful. Even though he knew the reasons why he had gone to Manhattan and that they'd made sense to him at the time, he now wondered why he'd left her behind.

You're an idiot.

"Come on." She took his hand and led him out of the lab. They slipped on their winter jackets and Charlotte jammed a furry toque down far on her head and wound her scarf around her face.

"It's not far, is it?" Quinn asked. "No dog sleds are needed?"

"No," Charlotte replied, despite being muffled under her thick scarf. "Just a short jog."

He hoped so. He wasn't enjoying the frigid temperatures of the Arctic. She opened the door and he was hit by a blast of icy air. He should've been used to it by now, but the low temperatures still surprised him.

They said nothing to each other as they shuffled through town to a little shack near the hangar. A steady stream of exhaust fumes floated up from the chimney—the aroma of old-fashioned cooking.

He could smell fries and his stomach growled at the thought of poutine. He was so hungry he might just take Mrs. Kamuk up on her offer to eat muktuk.

Chimes over the door jingled and they stomped their feet on the mat to shake off the snow. When he looked up, the patrons of the restaurant were all staring in wide-eyed wonder and Quinn felt like a specimen under examination at that moment.

"I should've mentioned that this diner is run by the Tikivik family," Charlotte whispered as she hung up her coat.

"Ah, so these are the hordes that were waiting in your clinic when I arrived yesterday?"

Charlotte nodded. "Yep, that would be them." She turned and waved and the group waved back then returned to their regular restaurant chatter.

"Do we wait for someone to seat us?" Quinn asked, looking around.

"It's not that kind of place, Devlyn." She took his hand again and his blood heated at her gentle touch. She led him to a corner booth and they slid into it. He sat down across from her. Charlotte handed him a vinyl-covered menu.

It was one sided and a bit smeared. She laughed as he held it with disdain. "The food is safe, Devlyn. You're hungry, I'm tired and you can't cook."

"Right. This stuff has to be better." Only his mind began to wander to the disgusting conversation with George earlier. If he continued thinking like that he wouldn't be able to eat anything.

Charlotte nodded and glanced at the menu.

"Ah, so the two doctors are gracing us with their presence tonight."

Quinn looked up at the pretty young waitress, who was the spitting image of Mentlana.

"Hey, Lucy. You haven't met Dr. Quinn Devlyn. Dr. Devlyn, this is Mentlana's twin, Lucy."

"Pleasure." He nodded.

"So, what'll it be tonight, Charley? Usual?"

"Yep."

Lucy nodded and looked expectantly at him. "What can I get for you, Dr. Devlyn?"

"What is a usual?"

Lucy chuckled. "A BLT, a salad and a diet cola."

"Sounds good, but make mine with fries. Oh, do you do poutines here?"

Lucy grinned. "Of course."

"Then that's what I'll have."

She nodded and headed back to the kitchen.

"I forgot about your affinity for poutines, Quinn. I guess you don't get many of those in Manhattan."

"Only on lunch breaks. Dinner out was more...a bit more top of the line."

"Escargots and the like?"

"Dammit." Quinn banged the table.

"What?" Charlotte asked, stunned.

"I forgot to tell George about escargots. I bet he'd be seriously squicked out."

Charlotte laughed. "He knows. He's been to Toronto many a time. He's just having some fun with you."

"That little..." Quinn laughed.

"He likes you." Charlotte smiled. "I think it's nice."

Lucy placed their drinks in front of them, grinning before leaving discreetly again.

"So, what is your obsession with food today?" Charlotte asked, playing with the straw in her glass of diet soda. "Have you suddenly miraculously learned how to cook?" There was a sparkle of devilment in her eyes.

He leaned closer to her across the table. "Do you remember the time I tried to make hamburger and cheese out of the packet and used lard instead of butter?"

Charlotte choked on her water. "Yes. It was horrific. Epically horrific, in fact." She shuddered. "I think I repressed that memory."

Quinn laughed and reached for her hand. Charlotte's eyes widened in shock at his touch, but she didn't try to pull away. Her hand was so slender and gave off the illusion it was delicate, but really it was strong. She'd had such potential to become a brilliant surgeon. Only Charlotte hadn't wanted that.

She'd wanted to be a general practitioner. Her hand felt so snug in his. So warm. So right.

"Remember the time I tried to make brownies and they only baked around the edges."

There was a twinkle in her eye. "I remember. Hard as a rock around the edges."

"But soft and gooey in the unbaked center. I must have tried to cook those brownies for three hours."

"I remember," Charlotte whispered. "I remember the smell. I was going through such bad…" She trailed off. The mirth disappeared. She straightened her spine and pulled her hand away.

He knew why she'd retreated emotionally. Quinn had known when he'd been making those brownies that she had been going through horrid morning sickness. She had been on Diclectin because she hadn't been able to keep anything down. It had killed him to see her suffer like that. So sick.

He'd tried to bake the brownies to cheer her up and butter her up to go to Manhattan. That day, the day of the miscarriage, the day Charlotte had lost the baby, had been the day he had been offered the private practice and fellowship in Manhattan. The offer had come from Dr. Robert Bryce, one of the leading neonatal surgeons on the Eastern Seaboard, and Dr. Bryce had wanted him, but Charlotte had refused to leave the godforsaken North.

That's how he'd felt about it.

Godforsaken.

Now he wasn't so sure. Charlotte was happy, and a successful physician.

And he was lonely.

"Anyway, I remember."

"Here are your meals, Doctors. By the way, Jake said they're on the house."

"No," Charlotte said, shaking her head vehemently. "We can pay, Lucy. You tell him we'll pay."

Lucy smiled, that cute dimple like her sister's appearing in her cheek. "You know Jake. He won't take no for an answer." Lucy looked at him then, her black eyes shining with warmth. "You are saving his nephew and my nephew. Jake is Genen's brother."

Charlotte sighed. "Lucy."

"It's done, Doc Charley. Deal with it." Lucy left them.

"That's awfully generous of them." Quinn turned and waved to the man behind the counter, the man he presumed was Jake.

"It's his way of saying 'thank you.' Everyone up here is family. Mentlana and Genen's baby means so much to this community."

Quinn's stomach rumbled and he looked down at his poutine. The meaty smell of the gravy made his mouth water in anticipation. The fries were fresh cut and thick and it had been a long time since he had real, home-cooked poutine.

"Lucy is actually going to be leaving us after Mentlana has her baby," Charlotte said, spearing a piece of lettuce.

"Really? Where's she going?"

"To Hamilton, Ontario. She's training to become a midwife and a registered nurse. I'm hoping she returns to Cape Recluse. I could use her."

"Doesn't Cape Recluse have a midwife? You mentioned her."

Charlotte nodded, chewing. "Lorna is getting old and ready to retire. Besides, if Lucy becomes a nurse she'll have much more training and knowledge than Lorna did. Lorna was trained by her mother...Anernerk."

"Anernerk is an impressive woman. So, midwifery is a generational thing. Well, I don't mean to interfere, but what you really need is another physician up here."

Charlotte nodded. "I know, but we've had this conversation before."

"I know." Quinn took a bite of his poutine and it was absolute heaven. God, he loved cheese curd. So bad for the arteries, but he was enjoying every bite.

"What do you think of Jake's cooking?" Charlotte asked. There was a smug smile plastered across her face.

"My compliments to the chef, for sure."

"Does it beat out all those fancy Manhattan restaurants?"

"Some. I won't lie to you, Charlotte. New York is a gourmand's paradise."

She smiled. "Really? I suppose your favorite restaurant is some crazy-ass posh spot where all the 'it' crowd goes."

"Nope. But it does serve the best fettuccine in the world."

"Mmm. I do love fettuccine."

"I know." Quinn took her hand again. "Perhaps you'll go there someday."

Charlotte put her head to one side, staring at him. "Perhaps."

Then he heard it, the distant rumble of something, something that was stirring at the back of his mind. A sound he should have recognized instantly. Charlotte heard it, too, and pulled her hand away. She stood and looked out the windows of the diner, like the rest of the patrons. Her phone started buzzing and she cursed under her breath when she pulled it out.

Far off on the horizon he could make out the flashing lights of a chopper, and the closer it got the louder the spinning of its blades became.

"What in the world...?" Quinn asked, puzzled.

"I'll wrap up the rest of your food and bring it over to the clinic, Doc Charley," Lucy called.

"Wrap up our food?" Quinn asked.

"Medical. There's an emergency. That was the text I received," Charlotte said quickly, before dashing off to get her coat. Quinn got up and tried to get his coat on before Charlotte disappeared out the door into the bitter cold towards the landing strip.

He zipped up his parka and went after her as she ran to meet the helicopter, which was making a quick landing.

Quinn's heart beat in time with each revolution of the helicopter's blade. George appeared by Charlotte's side, a gurney ready as they ducked to avoid decapitation.

Quinn hovered to the side, wanting to do something but not quite sure how trauma scenes played out up here. He watched the transfer and watched the paramedics climb into the helicopter again. Charlotte and George carried the gurney through the snow towards the clinic with a man dogging their heels.

He ran to head them off, opening the doors to the clinic and flicking on the lights.

Charlotte paid him no attention and he heard the patient's moans of pain as they came closer. His throat constricted when he got a good look at the patient on the stretcher and the obvious swelling under her thick blankets.

He could tell what was happening just by the woman's grimace and her husband's pained expression. An expression he had seen far too often, in countless men and women in waiting rooms.

The woman on the gurney was in labor and about to give birth.

He was the only qualified obstetrician currently in Cape Recluse.

Now was his time to shine.

CHAPTER EIGHT

"How far apart are the contractions?" Quinn asked.

"The medic said every fifteen minutes," Charlotte responded.

Quinn helped her wheel the gurney into exam room one. It was the largest room she had, but still a bit of a tight squeeze. Charlotte had delivered babies on her own before, but usually at the patient's home with Lorna in attendance. And there hadn't been that many births up here in recent years. This baby, for better or for worse, was on its way. The eyes of the patient, Mrs. Grise, were wide with fright, her mouth a thin line and her face white with pain.

"I tried to get her to Iqaluit," the patient's husband said nervously. "I thought we had time. It's our first and the baby is three weeks early."

Quinn shook his head and let out a *tsk* of frustration at what he saw as the man's stupidity. Charlotte could tell by the look on his face what Quinn thought of the husband's assumptions.

"You should've taken her down weeks ago." Quinn snapped as they wheeled the patient over to the far side of the exam room and transferred her to the bed.

"I wouldn't let him," Mrs. Grise panted. "I didn't want to be alone."

"It's all right, Mrs. Grise—" Charlotte started.

"Rebecca," the woman interjected through her deep breathing. "Please, just Rebecca."

"Rebecca," Charlotte said soothingly. "I'm Dr. James and I'm going to do everything I can to ease your discomfort."

"If you wanted an epidural, I'm afraid there's no time. I'm sorry," Quinn said gently to the panicked woman. The patient was terrified, and he was being very gentle with her as they continued to prep.

She was amazed. When they had been doing their residency he had never been this calm and soothing with patients before.

"It's okay. No drugs. I'm ready," Rebecca said.

"You're sure?" Charlotte asked.

Rebecca nodded. "I want a natural birth."

"Dr. James, may I speak with you?"

Charlotte was stunned by Quinn's formality. This wasn't some big city hospital. This was a small clinic, her small clinic at the top of the world.

"What?" Charlotte asked, never taking her eyes off of the patient.

"Do you have the supplies in case of an emergency C-section?" Quinn whispered.

"Do you think her case warrants it?"

Quinn shrugged. "I don't know. I'm just being prepared."

"Yes. I have everything."

Quinn gave her a half smile. "Keep her comfortable and I'll handle the rest." He turned to walk away, but Charlotte gripped his arm.

"You know you won't get paid for this. I've delivered babies before."

"And I've delivered probably ten times the amount you have. As for payment, I don't care. This is an emergency."

She should fight it, throw him out of her clinic, only he was the specialist and she knew nothing about this patient. He was right and she was stunned he was willing to do this delivery with no compensation, something the Quinn Devlyn of five years ago wouldn't have been happy about.

Still, there was his hand to consider.

"Dr. James?" Mr. Grise said, his voice panicked.

"Everything is going to be fine. Dr. Devlyn is one of the best." Charlotte turned away from Quinn, silently handing him the reins of her clinic and praying to God she had made the right decision.

"Thank you," Rebecca whispered, as her husband squeezed her hand.

Charlotte stood back with George, feeling utterly useless.

"Is Lorna on her way?" Charlotte asked.

"Her contractions are coming close together," Quinn said. "Doesn't look like Lorna's going to get here in time. Are you allergic to latex, Rebecca?"

"No," she said. "Not allergic to anything."

"Good." Quinn turned to the sink and scrubbed his hands. Charlotte helped him by drying his hands and putting on a pair of gloves. Their eyes locked for a moment as he slipped his scarred hand into the glove. Charlotte couldn't help but wonder if he'd be able to deliver the baby. She'd watched him do exercises yesterday, had watched Anernerk massage his bad hand. Would his hand be strong enough to hold such a fragile life?

Step in.

Only she didn't. Charlotte didn't want to frighten Rebecca and she didn't want George to blab to anyone that she had doubts about Quinn, the man who was going to save Mentlana's baby's life.

Quinn sat on the rolling stool and Charlotte adjusted the lamp. There was no time for modesty.

Quinn preformed the internal. "Ten centimeters and fully effaced." He looked up at Rebecca and smiled encouragingly. "Time to start pushing. Bear down. Now."

Rebecca nodded and began to push, as George counted with Mr. Grise.

Charlotte stayed by Quinn's side, watching a new life enter the world.

Please, God. Please let it be an easy birth.

She'd never seen Quinn deliver a child before. He hadn't liked her to watch him during his residency and she'd been very busy with her own. But he was gentle as he urged Rebecca on. He guided the frightened woman through the birth with so much care and concern that Charlotte's heart fluttered, and in this moment she felt very connected to him. For all his talk about power and position it was evident he was just as passionate about health care and his profession as she was.

"Good. Take a deep breath and push. Hard, Rebecca. Hard." He was easing the baby's head out. "You're doing great, Rebecca. Again."

Charlotte smiled behind her mask as the top of the head began to appear. Doctoring in a remote community was never so rewarding as at this moment. And Quinn had always questioned her about why she hadn't specialized. Here, she had a taste of it all.

Rebecca screamed, a gut-wrenching cry of agony, and Charlotte didn't blame her. This moment was known as the "ring of fire" for a good reason.

"Scalpel," Quinn said. Charlotte handed him the blade and he made a small incision to control the tearing. His hand was strong and steady as he made the cut.

"Come on, Rebecca. One more good push and your baby will be here," Charlotte urged.

Rebecca grunted as the head passed easily and the rest of the baby slipped into Quinn's waiting hands.

"A girl," Charlotte announced as she stared in awe at the tiny little life so delicately cradled in Quinn's hands. His gaze locked on her. She saw a glimmer of envy and longing mirrored there. Hope flared somewhere deep inside her. The baby took her first lusty cry of life and Quinn looked away.

"Take the baby," he said, his hands shaking a bit. Charlotte grabbed a blanket and reached down to hold the squawking infant.

As she stared down at the baby, tears stung her eyes as she thought of her own lost child. Rebecca had been so brave having a baby up here, away from what most people considered civilization. Braver than she was, even for having a baby, something Charlotte was terrified to even entertain the notion of again because she couldn't bear the thought of losing another child.

Get a grip on yourself, Charlotte.

She carefully placed the baby on Rebecca's chest, and Quinn cut the cord once it had stopped pulsating. The proud father cuddled his new daughter while Quinn delivered the afterbirth and stitched Rebecca up.

"Good job, Dr. Devlyn and Mom." George grinned at the happy parents, but Charlotte could see they were oblivious to everything. Rebecca's gaze was focused on her crying, thriving baby.

She recorded the APGAR and rubbed ointment on the baby's eyes to reduce infection. After that she gingerly placed the baby on the scale.

"She's seven pounds eight ounces."

Charlotte then took measurements of the baby. When five minutes had passed she recorded the APGAR again and gave the baby a vitamin K injection. The hospital in Iqaluit could do the heel stick tomorrow.

Charlotte swaddled the baby and took her over to the proud parents. Rebecca's arms were outstretched, tears streaming down her red cheeks. The new mother nuzzled her baby eagerly. A pang of longing rocked Charlotte to her core.

Charlotte wanted that. More than anything. More than any fear of what might happen.

"Thank you, Dr. James."

"It's Charlotte. Everyone up here calls me Charley, though."

Rebecca grinned. "Charlotte. I like that name."

"I think it's a perfect name for her," Quinn smiled. "I've always loved that name."

Charlotte blushed and smiled at Quinn. His eyes were twinkling and for a moment it was like the years had never separated them, that the hurt was forgotten. He returned her smile before turning away with the tray of instruments and medical waste.

"You can rest the night here, Mr. and Mrs. Grise. We'll take care of you, and tomorrow George or I will fly you down to Iqaluit. We'll need to notify the hospital that you've given birth here."

Rebecca nodded. "Thank you, Doctor... Thank you, Doc Charley."

"My pleasure." Charlotte peeled off her gloves and began to scrub. "George, make sure you set up a recovery room for them. I think there's a bassinet here. I always have stuff on hand. There's also some diapers and formula, if needed, in the supply room."

"I'm on it." George seemed to hesitate as he began to place instruments on a tray to be sterilized. "What happened to Dr. Devlyn?" he asked in whispered undertone.

"He's right..." Charlotte trailed off as her eyes scanned the room. He'd disappeared. "Probably went to clean up. He's done his job."

"Of course. He was fantastic. It gives me hope he'll help Mentlana." George's voice shook at the mention of his sister.

A lump formed in Charlotte's throat. "You okay to fly to Iqaluit tomorrow?" she asked, changing the subject.

"Yep. My schedule is free."

"Good."

She left the room and shut the door. Taking a deep breath, she slid down to the floor. Her knees were knocking and exhaustion hit her in waves. Emotions and adrenaline were still rushing through her. It had been watching Quinn hold the baby that had brought back a flood of emotions she'd thought long gone. He had been so tender, for a man who had always insisted he didn't want or particularly like kids, which had never made sense to her, given his chosen specialty.

The door to the clinic opened and Lorna shuffled in. Her face was haggard and she looked worn out.

"Am I too late?"

Charlotte stood, her body protesting. "Healthy baby girl. Sorry for dragging you out of bed."

Lorna shook her head. "No problem. I'll be glad when Lucy leaves soon to study midwifery. I'm getting too…"

"Tired. You're ready to retire." Charlotte offered.

Lorna smiled. "You're just too polite to say old, Charlotte."

"You're not old. Your mother, Anernerk, is old."

"I'll be sixty-eight soon, well past retirement age." Lorna slumped down in the waiting-room chair and Charlotte sat across from her.

"You can crash here for the night instead of trudging back home."

Lorna smiled weakly. "I just might take you up on that offer, help the new parents out and give you some rest."

"Thanks. Even though I was nothing more than a glorified nurse, it was an amazing experience."

"Does it make you change your mind?"

Charlotte dragged her hand through her hair. Lorna knew about her miscarriage and how Charlotte felt about becoming pregnant again. Charlotte blamed herself for losing the child. She had been an intern and had taxed her body way beyond its limits.

That's why she'd lost her baby.

"No," she answered uncertainly.

As the only doctor for kilometers around she was just as stressed, and she wouldn't lose another baby. She couldn't. It would kill her.

On the other hand, holding that baby tonight and watching

Quinn cradling that tiny little life with all the care in the world had made her rethink the decision she'd made five years ago.

If she was given the chance to carry and have another baby, she'd do so in a heartbeat.

Lorna arched an eyebrow. "There is uncertainty there."

Charlotte shook her head and stood. "I'll make you up a bed in the other recovery room."

Lorna shook her head. "Avoiding a touchy subject. Obstinate."

"You know, you sounded just like your mother, then." Charlotte chuckled and walked down the hall.

"Low, blow, Doc Charley. Really low blow. I'm old enough to be your mother."

"Keep talking…Anernerk."

Lorna let out a guffaw as Charlotte disappeared round the corner to the recovery room. She made up Lorna's room and could hear George making up the other one. Charlotte helped him settle the happy parents and the baby in the larger recovery room, the one usually used to house two patients, and got Lorna settled in the room opposite.

It was quite handy because Lorna was well versed in postpartum needs and she said she would keep watch on the new mother and baby during the night.

George collapsed on the waiting-room couch and was snoring by the time Charlotte finished sterilizing the instruments and cleaning the exam room, not wanting Rosie to have a heart attack when she came in on Monday.

As Charlotte closed down and turned off the lights, she stared at the door that connected to her home. It was slightly ajar and she could see the flicker of a television. Quinn was still awake.

She wanted to see him, to wrap her arms around him and kiss him. To finish what had almost started earlier today, but fear froze her in her tracks.

No. She couldn't deal with him tonight.

Instead, she grabbed her dinner, which had been parceled up from the diner, and wandered to her office, staring bleakly at the old couch that had adorned their apartment. Her eyes were heavy and the couch was surprisingly inviting. She locked the door to her office, peeled off her clothes and settled down on the couch, covering herself with the afghan she'd draped over Quinn only a day ago.

She was absolutely exhausted and tried to drift off to sleep, but the damn blanket smelled like him.

CHAPTER NINE

SHOUTING ROUSED CHARLOTTE from her slumber. She stumbled to her feet and the container from dinner last night fell onto the floor, scattering a few fries onto the carpet. One squished under her foot when she stepped forward and it stuck to her sock in a cold, mushy clump, making her curse under her breath.

Charlotte hopped on one foot to peer out the window. She gasped, not because it was snowing, which it was. It was the sight of Quinn outside in the snow that made her voice catch in her throat.

Quinn's outside? Voluntarily?

He was kneeling down and in his hand appeared to be a very expensive camera with a large telescopic lens. The shouting was from some of the village kids, who were rocketing past him from the slope just outside her office.

The clinic was on the far edge of town, nestled up against a slope, and because there were no houses on the one side, the village kids loved to come over and toboggan on nice days. When it was snowing big fat fluffy flakes, it was not as bitterly cold out as it would usually be.

As a kid zoomed past Quinn, the camera would follow. He was photographing the children.

I never knew he liked photography.

Or children, for that matter.

A smile quirked her lips as he moved the camera and urged a large sled of five kids down the hill. The children were laughing and he was making funny faces as the child at the back pushed off.

Quinn cheered and disappeared behind the camera, getting ready to take his picture. Charlotte was extremely attracted to this side of him, a side she'd never been privileged to see before. Watching him out there now with the village kids warmed her heart.

She left her office, changed her mushy sock, and freshened up quickly. She had her winter gear on in no time flat and was out the door to join him. There was no way she was going to miss this opportunity.

There was no wind and it wasn't bitterly cold when she stepped outside. It was just a nice winter day, with soft flakes floating down.

"Watch out, Doc!" Charlotte jumped back as a sled full of laughing kids whizzed past her. Quinn stood and grinned at her, his cheeks rosy from the cold.

"Good morning, or should I say, afternoon?"

"What time is it?" She'd been in such a rush to get outside she hadn't checked the time.

"It's one. Hey, hold up, guys. Doctor coming through." Quinn held up his hands and the eager tobogganers paused, but with a few "Awwws" as Charlotte jogged across the path of danger to stand beside Quinn. "All right, go, guys!"

With a shriek from one of the kids, the next sled set off and Quinn snapped a few shots as it whizzed by.

"I'm impressed," Charlotte said.

"By what?"

"You, out here in the *dreaded* ice and snow."

Quinn chuckled and he capped his camera lens. "I couldn't resist it."

"I didn't know you did photography."

Quinn shrugged. "It's no big deal. I dabble a bit." He

shielded the glare of the sun from the screen on the back and flicked through the images. They were beautiful photographs of the kids and other scenery. He'd also managed to take a shot of the northern lights. It was a stunning photograph that captured the green-and-purples hues of the aurora borealis dancing over the village.

"These are beautiful. When did you take that?" she asked, pointing to the image.

"Last night. You know, I've never seen the aurora borealis. I never bothered when we lived in Yellowknife, and when I was in Manhattan I kicked myself constantly for not making the time." Quinn switched off his camera. "Light pollution in the big city sucks."

"What time did you get up?" she asked, changing the subject from the city, which was a point of contention between them.

"About nine. George was taking the Grises down to Iqaluit. He was going to wake you, but you looked so darned cute huddled up on that old couch, food scattered all over the place."

Charlotte groaned, embarrassed he'd caught her flaked out and vulnerable instead of poised and sophisticated. "Thanks for doing that."

"No problem." His eyes glinted as he watched the kids haul their sleds back up the hill. "You know, I've never tried that."

"What, tobogganing?"

Quinn shook his head. "Nope, never. My parents wouldn't take me or even buy me a sled."

"I thought your dad was very much into sports. At least, that's what you told me."

"Hockey, yes, sledding, no. You can't win a gold medal for sledding."

"You can for bobsledding," she teased.

Quinn shrugged. "He wasn't much for being a team player. I just had to be the best."

A pang of sympathy hit her. Quinn may have had two parents but he hadn't had a fun childhood. Some of Charlotte's best memories of her and her father had been out on the snow, sledding and snowshoeing. Charlotte grabbed his hand and tugged him towards the hill. "We're going."

"What?" He chuckled. "You're nuts. What about my camera?"

"Jenny!" Charlotte called out to Wavell's younger sister. She came bounding up, out of breath.

"Yeah, Doc Charley?"

"Can you hold Dr. Devlyn's camera while I take him on your sled down the hill?"

Jenny's face broke into a huge smile. "Yeah, I can do that!"

"Charlotte…" Quinn started as she took the camera from him and handed it to Jenny. "I don't know."

"Come on, you big wimp!"

He raised his eyebrows. "Wimp, eh?"

She screeched as he lunged for her. She grabbed Jenny's small sled and ran up the hill, Quinn following her. When they reached the top she sat down. "Sit behind me and hold on."

"How do we push off?" he asked as he sat down, his arms wrapping around her.

"With your feet. But once we're going, tuck them up so your feet don't slow us down."

"Gotcha."

"Ready?" she asked.

"Yep. Let's get this over with."

Charlotte could hear the kids shrieking and laughing as she dug her feet in and pushed off. The sled picked up speed fast from their combined weight and they rocketed down the hill, past Jenny and the clinic. Charlotte screamed with pure joy as the wind whipped at her face and the cold air sucked the breath from her lungs.

Quinn yelled and stuck his feet out as they headed towards the only road in Cape Recluse. The sled careened to the side and they were tossed out. Charlotte did a small roll and landed on her back. Quinn rolled and landed on top of her, pinning her to the snow.

"Are you all right?" he asked breathlessly. "And my apologies for the excessive bad language."

Charlotte couldn't stop laughing. "I'm fine."

"I think I like this sledding business." He grinned down at her, his dark eyes twinkling. "You've popped my cherry twice since I've been here."

Heat spread through her like wildfire, while her body zinged with arousal. His body was heavy, pressed against hers, but it was the kind of weight she was longing for. If only all these layers of clothing weren't separating them. If only they were in her bed, naked.

She sobered instantly when she realized Quinn was still lying on top of her, in front of her clinic, in front of the village children. She could hear them laughing.

"Hey, you're too heavy. Get off me, already!"

Quinn shifted and rolled over. She scrambled to her feet and brushed the snow from her. "I'd better go change. I'm not wearing any snow pants and my jeans will be soaked in a few minutes."

She spun round and ran for the clinic, not looking back. She'd forgotten for a moment that he was not her fiancé. He wasn't anything to her anymore. Just a colleague, up here for a consult.

Quinn retrieved his camera from Jenny and bid his new fan club farewell. The sun would be setting soon and the kids had to head for home. Besides, his hand was numb from the cold, but, like he'd told Charlotte, he hadn't been able to resist the photographic opportunity.

When he was back in his bedroom he scrolled through the

pictures and saw one of him and Charlotte, racing down the hill. It seemed that Jenny was a bit of a photo aficionado, as well. He didn't mind in the least. It was something to remember that moment by.

He thought Charlotte's cold reserve was melting a bit. She was playful and laughing again, but when they had been lying in the snow, something had clicked. He'd seen it in her eyes and her barriers had gone up again. He turned off the camera and set it down.

A zing of pins and needles shot up his arm. Quinn stared down at his scarred hand and flexed it. It wasn't as stiff as it had been. His hand had been steady and sure when he'd made the episiotomy. He'd seen the look on Charlotte's face when she'd helped him put the gloves on, the moment of uncertainty. He wasn't a fool. Quinn knew she'd seen the scars. He wanted to tell her about the accident and reassure her there was nothing to be worried about, though his mother would beg to differ.

Quinn scrubbed his hand over his face and picked up his hand exerciser, clenching his hand into a tight fist and then slowly allowing it to flex again.

"You'll never regain full use of your hand. I would suggest you open up a consultation practice or move into a general practice instead of surgery, Dr. Devlyn," the orthopedic surgeon said.

"I don't accept that."

"Quinn, see sense. Even Dr. Szarsky thinks you won't be able to continue to be a surgeon. When will you listen to reason?" his mother lamented. "You had such potential, too."

"I still have potential. I'm still a surgeon."

"Perhaps," his father said. "But it'll take about a year at the minimum to recuperate. By then you'll have lost your professional edge."

"Like I lost mine having you!"

His mother's tone had been so hard and cold when she had uttered those words, *I lost mine having you.* Quinn shook those horrible memories away. His parents had never been support-ive except when he'd excelled.

Mediocrity had never been an option.

Except with Charlotte.

Charlotte had never judged him when he'd had a minor set-back. She'd always cared for and loved him, no matter what he'd done, and had cheered him on to do better next time, without any hint of malice or remorse.

A slow-paced life in a rural clinic or a small-town hospi-tal was what he'd secretly craved since his accident, but he'd never admitted to it because he could've had that with Char-lotte, and Quinn never admitted his mistakes.

He cursed under his breath and set the hand exerciser on the nightstand. He got up and splashed some water on his face at the basin. When he glanced in the mirror he saw a thick growth of stubble and dark circles under his eyes. He hadn't slept well. Every time he'd closed his eyes, all he'd seen had been Charlotte.

In that moment when he'd passed the baby to her it had been like their painful past and their separation had been washed away. Back then, all he'd wanted had been his parents' ap-proval. Once he'd achieved what they'd wanted from him, it still hadn't been good enough, and when his father had died he'd realized it never would be.

Just like he'd realized as soon as he'd left Charlotte that there would be no going back. He'd lost her trust.

Yet that look they shared… That moment of connection had seemed so genuine, so real, and he'd felt like he'd never been away, that they were right back to where they'd started. Of course, he could've just been seeing things. Charlotte had made it pretty clear when he'd arrived that their association was going to remain purely professional.

If he had the chance to start all over again with Charlotte, would he?

Damn straight, he would.

His phone chimed with the familiar sound of a text message coming through. Quinn groaned and picked his phone up from the nightstand. Only two people would be texting him. It would be either the hospital or his mother, and Quinn had a gut-wrenching feeling it wasn't the hospital.

As he glanced at the screen he recognized the area code of Toronto. Two words were on the screen.

Call me.

Quinn rolled his eyes. He knew why she was doing this. She knew where he was and she didn't approve. Not one bit. His mother wasn't impressed in the least that he was giving a pro bono consult, especially for a patient of Charlotte's.

His phone vibrated in his hand.

What could possibly be so important you can't call your mother to discuss an urgent matter? I bet you would've called if it was your father.

Quinn rolled his eyes. His mother was laying on the guilt trip pretty thick—another aspect of his childhood he hadn't particularly enjoyed, being the pawn between his parents. His mother had been a master of guilt. "Had" being the operative word.

He really couldn't care less. Instead, he called his physiotherapist. He wanted reassurance.

"Ted Jones speaking."

"Hey, Ted. It's Devlyn."

There was a pause. "Devlyn! How's it up there?" Ted asked pleasantly.

"Cold."

"I bet." Ted chuckled. "How's the hand?"

"Stiff, sore. The usual." Quinn scrubbed his hand over his

face, preparing himself mentally for what he wanted to ask, dreading the answer. "My hand, do you think...? Will I regain full use of it?"

You can't avoid him for the rest of the day.

Charlotte groaned. Her conscience pricking her, she'd spent a most uncomfortable night on the couch in her office because of her conflicted emotions about Quinn. She was still wearing the same clothes as yesterday and now her jeans were soaked.

As much as she wanted to go and talk to Quinn about what had happened out in the snow, she couldn't will herself to do it. It was like her body was frozen to the spot, some sort of primeval defense mechanism to prevent her from facing Quinn and appearing like a schmuck in front of him, thus protecting her heart from further injury.

At least, that's what she kept trying to tell herself she was doing.

Really, she knew deep down she was being a coward.

"That's it." She quickly changed out of her wet clothes. She couldn't hide out in her bedroom. She was going to face Quinn and see where the chips fell.

When she opened her bedroom door she heard his raised voice filter through from the guest bedroom.

"Honestly, tell me the truth, Ted."

Quinn sounded agitated and worried.

Charlotte tiptoed down the hall. The door to his bedroom was slightly ajar. She could just catch a glimpse of Quinn sitting at the desk, holding his head in his hands and staring down at the phone, which was on speaker.

"I really can't say, Quinn. I'm only stating the facts from what I've seen in other cases."

Her heart skipped a beat. *Cases? What cases?*

"I need some kind of a ballpark idea, Ted. Just give me that. It'll put my mind at ease."

There was a loud audible sigh over the phone. "No, you

probably won't regain full function of your hand again. Your hand was crushed. You're lucky you still have it and have some range of motion."

This time her heart didn't skip a beat. It almost stopped completely. The blood was draining away from her face and the room began to spin.

Couldn't. Operate? The implications were too horrific to fathom.

She wanted to move away. Her stomach was knotting, her throat was constricted as she fought the urge to be sick. All she could think about was Mentlana and the baby. He was risking her reputation, as well. If Mentlana or the baby died because he failed to mention he was no longer fit for duty, her reputation would be on the line. The people of Cape Recluse wouldn't trust her as freely as they did now.

His ineptitude could cost her the only home she'd ever known, and that thought was too frightening.

There was no way she was going to risk her family, the people she loved, because Quinn's pride might be hurt. If he couldn't operate then there was no way he was going near Mentlana Tikivik, or anyone else, for that matter. But she also felt sorry for Quinn. His whole focus in med school had been about becoming the best, the top of his field, and now he couldn't operate. How must he feel about that?

"Can I operate?" Quinn asked.

"I don't see why not, but you'll most likely need assistance."

"I don't have access to other surgeons."

"Look, I could say you'd be fine, but without assessing your hand I can't give you a definite answer. Just keep up with the exercises.

"Thanks, Ted."

"Call me if you need some more help. Sorry I couldn't ease your mind."

Charlotte heard Quinn end the call and shut off his phone.

She tried to move away from where she was standing, but once again she was frozen to the spot.

Quinn whipped open the door and his eyes widened as he saw her, standing still in the hallway, shaking with anger and betrayal. It was her own fault. She'd allowed him into her life again. At least this time she hadn't lost a baby. At least this time her heart hadn't been blown to smithereens.

"Charlotte." His tone was weary and he rubbed the back of his neck. "I didn't know you were here."

"No," she said quickly. "No. I don't suppose you did."

CHAPTER TEN

"CHARLOTTE..." QUINN'S HEART stuttered at the sight of her. She was dressed casually in a soft-looking lavender sweater and blue jeans, her red curls hanging loose over her shoulders. Her posture, however, was anything but casual, and her face was like thunder. She stood like she was on the edge of a precipice, and that one wrong move by him and she'd jump.

"Well?" she asked.

"Charlotte, I wanted to tell you. It's been something I've been trying to tell you since I arrived."

Her gaze dropped to his hand and the scars that marred the surface of his skin. He was sure she was looking past the physical ones he carried to the ones deep inside him and the haunted past that had scarred them both, and he watched as the anger in her face ebbed away.

"Tell me," she urged gently, at last.

Do not be the obstinate man.

He met Charlotte's gaze. Though her face was now unreadable and passive, her eyes were full of concern. He longed to pull her into his arms once more, to tell her everything would be okay.

Only he didn't know how to say the words, or if it would all be okay.

"Quinn, please."

"I'm still a surgeon, if that's what you're wondering. I have a medical license." It was all he could say. He was having a hard time trying to tell her that his hand had been broken. It would be like admitting his own defeat, admitting to her that he was the shadow of his former self.

"Okay," she said, confused. "I assumed so. Tell me about the scars, Quinn. What happened?"

"A car accident."

She nodded. "Go on."

"Fog caused a massive pileup on the highway. My car flipped, my hand became lodged in the door. For a while I didn't think it could be saved. Hell, when I was trapped, waiting for the paramedics, I thought I was going to die."

Charlotte's face paled and she moved into his bedroom. "Why didn't you tell me this before?"

"You brought me up here to operate on your friend. I couldn't tell you what had happened to me."

"So putting Mentlana's life at risk is not as important as saving face?"

"Of course not!" he snapped, and then took a deep breath as he sat down on the edge of his bed. "I'd never put a patient at risk. It's why I was calling my physiotherapist."

Charlotte closed the distance between them and sat next to him, taking his shattered hand in hers.

"If your physiotherapist or orthopedic surgeon cleared you for surgery and you still have your license, you can operate." It was if she was stating it because she couldn't quite believe it, and he didn't blame her one bit.

"Yes" was all he said.

"You know you can, or else you wouldn't have boarded that plane and come up here."

What if I came up here for purely selfish reasons? Which was what he wanted to say, but didn't. Instead, he pulled his hand out of hers and stood.

"I won't put your friend's life at risk. I hope you can trust me on this. Do you trust me, Charlotte?"

* * *

Charlotte didn't know what to say. The room began to spin and she was still trying to take in everything. She knew something had happened to him, but didn't know the extent. She stood and turned her back to him, unable to process what he'd just asked. Did she trust him? She didn't even know that answer herself, so how could she tell him otherwise?

"I don't…I don't know what to say."

"You don't have to say anything. You have no reason to trust me. I deceived you. I didn't tell you about my accident, but I want you to know I'd never do anything to harm a patient."

Charlotte heard his footfalls as he closed the space between them, the heat of his body against her back as he stood behind her. She moved away, stunned and not sure she could believe him. If she did and he was wrong and something happened to Mentlana… The thought was too horrifying to comprehend.

She glanced over her shoulder and her heart skipped a beat, her stomach fluttering just looking at him. Charlotte nodded slowly. "I trust you."

"Thank you." Quinn moved past her to leave, but she reached out and took his hand again. He paused and she traced the faint scars with her thumb. She could only begin to imagine the hours of pain he'd endured as they'd put the pieces of him back together.

"I'm sorry I wasn't there to help you," she whispered.

He tilted her chin so she was forced to look at him. "You have nothing to apologize for."

Charlotte's knees began to knock just a bit as she stared into his eyes, getting lost in them. His eyes were like melted chocolate and she *so* loved chocolate.

It'd been so long since his strong arms had wrapped around her. His absence in her life was akin to physical pain. A pain that had been numbed by throwing herself into her work and reminding herself of the pain he'd caused her.

Quinn's hand slipped around her neck, his fingers tangling in her hair at the nape, bringing her closer to him. His hot breath fanned her cheek. She closed her eyes, waiting for the kiss that she didn't know she longed for, but which she did, all the same.

What am I doing?

Yeah, she trusted him in his surgical abilities, but she wasn't ready to let him into her heart again. She placed a hand on his chest, keeping him at bay. "I can't. The day you left was the worst day of my life. I lost you and I lost..." She trailed off, not wanting to share the pain of losing their child. She'd borne it alone for so long.

He nodded. "I understand. I'm just grateful you trust me to do right by your friend. Thank you."

Charlotte turned on her heel and left his room. He'd gotten to her again and she'd almost let down her guard.

She hated how he affected her so.

Charlotte avoided Quinn as much as possible. She was angry at herself for momentarily allowing him to break through to her and she was angry that her hormones seemed to be over-ruling her common sense.

Of course, it was hard to block Quinn out of her life when they only had two thousand square feet of combined clinic and house space. Add that to a blinding blizzard that lasted three days, keeping them housebound.

At least she had her regular work to keep her busy, when patients desperate enough were able to slog through the snow to keep their appointments. Most of her day was dealing with her job, locked in her office with only the roar of the storm outside to accompany her and her jangled thoughts.

Alone in her office, she kept reliving their doomed relationship over and over again. After it had ended, when she'd first looked back on it, she'd chastised herself for not noticing that things would never have worked out between them.

And it hadn't only been about their very different career paths. Quinn wasn't a family man. That was one thing that hadn't changed about him. Charlotte wanted a family, more than anything, and Quinn was a workaholic.

When and if she ever did meet Mr. Right, she wanted to provide two parents for her children. Charlotte wanted to give them what she'd never had.

"Doc Charley?" Charlotte looked up to see George standing in the doorway.

"Yeah, what can I do for you?"

"Closing time." A smile spread across George's face.

Charlotte glanced at the clock on her computer monitor and balked. The afternoon had flown by. She had still been working on Wavell's file, although she had pulled out the boy's sutures earlier that day.

"Have a good night," she said absently.

"It's bingo night at the community center. You up for some B.I.N.G.O?" George asked, enunciating every letter in an annoying way.

Charlotte shook her head. "I don't relish going out in that storm."

"Storm ended hours ago, Charley," George said, confused. "You must've been really engrossed in filing if you didn't even notice the silence."

Charlotte shook her head. No, she hadn't noticed the howling wind had stopped. She'd grown so accustomed to the deafening sound that she hadn't even noticed that it had ended. Apparently she truly had zoned out, because the coffee in her cup from that morning was stone cold and the cup was still full. She dropped the file and scrubbed a hand over her face.

"Are you all right, Charley?" George asked, concerned.

"Fine. Just a bit tired." She bit her lip, hoping George wouldn't see through her lie. If he did, he didn't say anything.

"Come out to the community center. Everyone is coming

tonight for bingo, a way to celebrate the storm being over. I'm even going to fetch Aanak and drag her in."

A smile tugged at the corners of her lips. "No, thanks. I think I'll keep up with my filing. Besides, I hate bingo."

George shook his head. "Suit yourself. I guess it's just me and Doc Devlyn, then."

"Quinn's going?" Charlotte was stunned. Absolutely and utterly flabbergasted. Quinn was not the community-center, bingo-card-stamping type. Except for formal mixers, Quinn had never gone out with the other students, unless it had been with her.

"Yep." There was a twinkle to George's eye. "He said he's really looking forward to it."

Now she *had* to go. She wouldn't miss seeing this for the world. "Well, I guess I can come out, seeing that Anernerk will be there and everything."

George grinned. "Ri-i-ight. You're going because Aanak will be there."

Charlotte frowned. "What exactly are you implying? And tread carefully."

"Nothing. Nothing." George held up his hands and backed out of the room. Charlotte chuckled to herself when he'd disappeared. He knew not to mess with her. He might be taller than her, but she could still give him a good noogie if she was so inclined.

She wasn't lying about wanting to see Anernerk, but the real show would be watching Quinn interacting with the townsfolk. He was not a natural people person. In fact, she knew he was only in the medical profession because it'd been forced on him by his parents, and she couldn't help but wonder what his chosen profession would've been if he'd had the choice.

He'd never had hobbies when they'd been together, other than traveling. He'd liked to see new places and had often talked about the trips he wanted to take. Perhaps he would've taken up photography.

Was that why he was taking it up now, as a fallback because of his hand injury? Charlotte groaned, annoyed with herself for expending so much thought on Quinn Devlyn. His life, his choices were not her concern anymore. Once he did his job up here she was over 100 percent positive he'd be on the next flight to Toronto.

Back to his job at the hospital in the big city and working as much as he could to stay at the top of his game.

And that was a bet she could take to the bank.

CHAPTER ELEVEN

THE COMMUNITY CENTER was packed and blaring out music. Charlotte handed her coat to the young girl behind the coat check.

"You'd better hurry up, Doc Charley. They've already started the first round," the young girl said.

"Thanks, Lizzie."

Charlotte hadn't gone over with George and Quinn as she'd had to make a house call on a sick patient, the only resident in Cape Recluse, besides Mentlana and Genen, who wasn't in attendance at bingo tonight. Besides, Charlotte was in no rush. She wanted to watch Quinn from afar to see how he interacted with the residents.

She'd been so shocked when George had told her Quinn had agreed to go. This was one bingo night she wasn't going to miss for the world. She lingered in the doorway of the main auditorium and easily picked out Quinn, near the back and by himself.

His brow was furrowed as he was bent over the cards. A smile touched her lips. They'd suckered him out of at least twenty bucks because he had about four cards sprawled out in front of him and he couldn't keep up with marking his tickets with the chips.

"He sucks. Big time."

Charlotte turned to see Anernerk at the table beside the

door. Anernerk was a pro at bingo. She could carry on any kind of conversation without missing a beat.

"What do you mean?"

Anernerk snorted. "He sucks. What more is there to say?"

"B seven."

"Boo!" Anernerk shouted. "Call something good for a change."

Charlotte stifled a laugh. Poor George was the caller and sent his dear, sweet Aanak a withering look, but only because Anernerk was engrossed in her bingo cards.

"You think I should go help him?" Charlotte asked.

"Yeah, but if you win…" Anernerk sent her a brief but silent warning.

Charlotte just grinned and made her way round to where Quinn was seated. "Having fun?"

Quinn glanced up and then laughed. "No. I think George should've been an auctioneer instead of a bingo caller."

Charlotte took the empty seat next to him and aided Quinn in catching up. "He's neither. He's a paramedic. They're trained to move quickly."

"Well, his training in this situation is not needed," Quinn grumbled.

"You wish he was slower in this case?" she teased.

"Of course," Quinn said, as he placed another chip. "I'm a novice. I was promised a night of cheap fun."

"Cheap fun? You're in the wrong town for *cheap* fun."

Quinn grinned and then chuckled. "Well, I'm used to attending soirees where plates go for at least fifty dollars and up."

"It's all relative, I guess." Charlotte placed another chip. "There, you've caught up now."

"For now." Quinn cursed under his breath as George called out three more numbers in rapid succession. "Drat. I'm literally all thumbs tonight."

"Slow it down, you!" Charlotte called out, trying not to laugh.

George raised his eyebrows in question and then spied Charlotte. He shook his head and continued in his normal tempo of firing off numbers.

"Hey, you heard the doctor. Slow it down or else." This time the demand came from Anernerk and this time George dared not ignore the request.

Quinn was stifling his laughter. "She's a bit intense about this game."

"She's competitive."

"I see where you got it from," Quinn said.

"What do you mean?"

Quinn rolled his eyes. "Oh, come on. You were out for blood at medical school. Always had to be top in the class, win every competition and every scholarship. It was damn annoying."

Charlotte glared at him, but saw the mirth in his eyes and retracted her claws a bit. "All right, I'll give you that. So, if I was *so* annoying, why did you pursue me?"

She regretted the question the moment it had left her lips when she saw the dark, hungry glint in his eyes, a look that caused warmth to spread through her body. She almost forgot where she was. Charlotte felt like that giddy med student in anatomy class, shyly watching Quinn on the other side of the classroom.

"G fifty-eight."

Quinn tore his gaze from her and set down a chip. "Damn, I think I won. Did I?"

Charlotte leaned over. "You did. You'd better call it."

"Bingo!" Quinn yelled out, standing up waving his card, letting the chips scatter everywhere. "Damn."

"Forfeit! He dropped his chips!" Anernerk said loudly, with a hint of triumph in her voice.

Charlotte couldn't control her laughter, then. She got down

on her knees and began to retrieve the bingo chips from the floor. Quinn got down and helped her.

"Anernerk is right."

"How's that?" Charlotte asked, setting a fistful of chips on the table.

"I do suck."

Quinn took a swig of his soda and leaned against the bar in the community center. He used the word "bar" loosely as it only served sodas, coffee and tea. He had excused himself from this round of bingo and had left Charlotte to hold down the fort.

In spite of Anernerk's protests, he had still won because they could track the previous numbers called.

It surprised him how much he enjoyed the game and socializing with the people in the community. That snowstorm had lasted for what had felt like an eternity. He was Canadian and used to blizzards, but nothing of this magnitude and ferocity. But then again, he'd grown up in a city, and tall buildings did serve a good use as windbreaks against whiteouts and squalls.

There was nothing here, no trees, just water on all sides and a mountain of rock, ice and snow behind the town. They were certainly at the mercy of the elements here. It was raw and powerful and for the first time he actually understood the reason why Charlotte loved it up here.

Quinn shook his head and ran his fingers through his hair. Perhaps the deafening roar of that snowstorm had addled his brain.

One thing not confusing him was how much he was enjoying his time with Charlotte. After he'd told her what had happened to him, she'd kept her distance from him. A tense silence had fallen between them and it saddened him. She ate her meals in her office and their only conversations were just cursory politenesses or talking about Mentlana's case.

He was used to silence, but he'd been alone for far too

long. When he'd arrived in Cape Recluse he hadn't realized how hungry for company he'd been, especially for Charlotte's.

He'd missed her, but he'd never really let it sink in how much. Being back in her presence reminded him of it, keenly.

Quinn didn't know what had changed and why the tense barrier that had fallen between them these last few days was gone, but he was thrilled. She seemed to be enjoying herself immensely, even though George told him she never usually came to bingo as she didn't particularly enjoy it.

Charlotte was beaming from ear to ear and she was very at ease with the people, and they with her. It was like they were family—for all intents and purposes, they were. He envied Charlotte that she really loved what she was doing.

Here she shone like the bright star she was.

Quinn had never seen her like this. Five years ago, in Yellowknife, he hadn't seen any job prospects, any chance for advancement. He'd thought of Canada's North as a dead-end career, but it wasn't.

He'd been so wrong.

He'd been too hasty when he'd left.

Watching Charlotte now, he was regretting the decisions he'd made.

"Are you going to play the next round, Devlyn?"

Quinn turned to see Anernerk beside him. She looked a bit frailer then when he'd first laid eyes on her a few days earlier. He hoped, for Charlotte's sake, that nothing was seriously wrong with her, but then, the old gal *was* over a hundred.

"Well, are you?" Anernerk winked at him.

"I may," Quinn conceded.

"I like competition. Especially, fresh meat."

"I believe your grandson remarked on that the first time I met you."

"He knows me well." Anernerk smiled and then picked up his bad hand. "Has it been troubling you much?"

"No, not too much. The blizzard caused a bit of an ache."

Anernerk nodded. "Your hand is steady enough. I wouldn't worry."

Quinn cocked an eyebrow. "I'm not. Not in the least."

Liar.

"I see," she said carefully. She released his hand and then shook her finger at him. "I'm going to get you next round. You had beginner's luck, but I think that's run out. I shall have victory."

Anernerk hobbled off and Quinn trailed after her, sitting next to Charlotte and sliding a can of ginger ale across to her.

"Milady," he said, giving a little flourish with his hand.

"Thanks." Charlotte popped the top and stuck a straw in the can.

"How are we doing?" he asked.

"Not well, I'm afraid."

"O sixty-seven."

"Boo!" Quinn called out. "This game is rigged."

Charlotte snorted and several people laughed. George was shocked, but grinned and continued with the game.

"I'm shocked, Dr. Devlyn, by such a display," Charlotte teased.

"Are you thoroughly scandalized?"

"Of course."

Quinn chuckled. "Perhaps we should call it quits. Besides, Anernerk warned me that she'd have victory, or else."

"Well, in that case, we'd better leave while the going's good." Charlotte finished her soda and Quinn collected up the game paraphernalia and handed it back to the ladies who had persuaded him in the first place to buy four cards.

They retrieved their coats and headed out into the freezing night. The moment they stepped outside, a brilliant display of vibrant green aurora borealis erupted across the sky.

"I can't believe how I missed this during my year in Yellowknife." Quinn wasn't watching where he was going and lost his footing. Charlotte reached out and steadied him.

"I think you've had a bit too much pop tonight," she teased.

"Perhaps. Or my eardrums were shattered by that raging blizzard." He gazed at Charlotte, bundled up in her parka. All he could see was the twinkle in her eyes and the tip of her nose, and he fought the urge to lean forward and press a kiss there. Charlotte let go of her hold on him, though. The light-hearted jesting they shared at the community center had vanished, replaced once more by the uneasy tension.

"It's freezing out here." Charlotte laughed nervously and stepped back, jogging the rest of the short way back to her clinic.

Quinn followed, because it was freezing, but he didn't know what had changed again and he was sad that it had.

CHAPTER TWELVE

CHARLOTTE SPENT THE night tossing and turning, just like she'd spent the last several. Quinn had changed. When he'd first arrived, she hadn't been sure that he had. He'd still seemed like the same old workaholic who'd left her.

The Quinn who had shown himself to her now was a completely different man, a man she only caught glimpses of when they were alone together away from prying eyes. A man he never allowed out in public. There were still shadows of his former self, but she was learning more about him. More than she'd ever thought possible.

Last night at bingo she'd thoroughly enjoyed herself.

Charlotte gave up any pretense of trying to sleep. She got up and dragged herself to the shower, using the last bit of hot water in her heater for the morning. She got dressed in warm layers as today she had to make a visit to Mentlana.

Quinn was nowhere in sight when she left her bedroom. She couldn't help but wonder where he was. He wasn't in the guest bedroom, because the door was wide open.

There was a pot of coffee waiting and a note from Quinn that stated he was out with George, ice fishing.

Ice fishing?

Charlotte pinched the bridge of her nose. Quinn had willingly gone out on the ice? With George?

She shook her head, filled her travel mug with some coffee and collected the items she'd need for Mentlana's checkup.

When she headed outside she could see a few brightly colored huts out on the water and she couldn't help but wonder which one Quinn was in. She could picture him bundled up, cursing at the stupidity of sitting out in the bitter cold, watching a hole for a bite on his pole.

Actually, what would be even better would be if a seal ended up popping up through Quinn and George's hole. That would certainly give him a fright. She'd be willing to endure a few hours of ice fishing just to see that.

"Quick lollygagging and get in here!" Anernerk was hanging out the doorway.

"What the heck are you doing here?" Charlotte asked. "More importantly, how the heck did you get here?"

"Genen picked me up last night from bingo. I just decided to stay here for a few days. I didn't think I was confined to my home." Anernerk pointed at her cheek.

Charlotte leaned over and gave her a kiss. "Well, since you're here, maybe I'll give you a checkup, too."

"Don't you dare!" Anernerk grinned and took Charlotte's coat. "Where's Dr. Devlyn today?"

"Ice fishing with George."

"Really? I'm impressed."

"What's going on out there?" Mentlana called out.

"You better go see her," Anernerk said. "She's going a bit squirrely, being on bed rest."

Charlotte walked down the hallway to Mentlana's bedroom. The television had been moved into the room. Actually, it looked like most of Mentlana's living room had been crammed into her small bedroom.

"How are you feeling today?" Charlotte asked.

"Don't patronize me." A smile quirked on Mentlana's lips. "Fill me in on all the gossip."

Charlotte set her bag down on the table and pulled out a blood-pressure monitor. "Gossip? There's no gossip."

Mentlana snorted. "Please."

Charlotte strapped the cuff on Mentlana's arm. "Please, what?"

"How has it been, working with Quinn?"

Charlotte groaned. Of course Mentlana had to ask that. How *had* it been, working with Quinn? Awkward at first, annoying at times and maddening as she had to constantly wrestle with her emotions, emotions she'd thought were long since buried.

"That good, huh?" Mentlana said, as Charlotte took her blood pressure.

Charlotte tapped her nose. The last thing she wanted to do was talk about it. "Your blood pressure is a little high. We'll keep an eye on it." She pulled out her portable Doppler to listen to the baby's heartbeat. She listened and didn't like the sound she heard. "Is Genen here?" she asked.

"What's wrong?"

Charlotte squeezed Mentlana's hand. "I'd like Genen to go out and get Dr. Devlyn for me. I just want him to listen to the baby's heartbeat, that's all."

"He's on the ice." Mentlana picked up her phone and texted him. "He's with George and Dr. Devlyn."

"Good." Charlotte wrote down the baby's irregular heartbeat. She'd have to get Mentlana in to the clinic for another ultrasound to check on the progress of the CCAM.

"Okay, you owe me gossip now that I'm all stressed until Dr. Devlyn gets here. Now, spill."

"There's nothing to spill."

Mentlana's gaze narrowed. "You can't fool me. You've been scarce, quiet and very unlike yourself. You've been locked away in your clinic for days."

"There was a snowstorm."

"I'm not talking just about the blizzard, Charlotte."

Charlotte sighed. "It's hard."

"Being around him?"

Charlotte nodded. "He left me."

Mentlana bit her lip. "You left him too, though."

"What do you mean? He went to New York. He picked his career over me."

"I know. His timing sucked when he left, but you didn't go with him, either. This is going to sound harsh, and I should really be careful, considering you're my doctor, but did you ever think about how he felt when you didn't go with him?"

Tears stung Charlotte's eyes. No. She never had considered his feelings, just like she'd never even considered following him to New York.

Both of them had been so stubborn, so pigheaded and set in their ways.

There had been no compromise. There never had been.

"I think you still care for him, Charlotte, even if you don't want to admit it, and I think you should give him another chance."

Charlotte wasn't sure she could. She was terrified to put her heart at risk again.

The door opened and she heard stamping by the door.

"Charlotte?" Quinn called out.

She cleared her throat, to knock the nervousness out. "In the bedroom."

Quinn opened the door, his face rosy from the cold, his hair tousled by the wind, and there was stubble on his chin. The dark green of his fisherman's sweater really brought out the dark brown of his eyes. He looked like he should be gracing the cover of some outdoor magazine. His appearance was rugged and it made the butterflies in her stomach flutter.

"Is everything okay?" he asked, a little out of breath.

"I need you to listen to the baby's heartbeat. Also, Mentlana's blood pressure is slightly elevated."

Quinn nodded. "Sure."

Charlotte stood up and let him sit down beside Mentlana. He used the Doppler, his brow furrowed in concentration as he listened to the heartbeat. After a couple of minutes he switched it off.

"Well?" Mentlana asked nervously.

"Your baby is fine. However, I'd like to do an ultrasound to check on him." Quinn stood. "Genen is on his way back. Have him bring you over to the clinic as soon as he can."

Mentlana nodded. "Okay."

Quinn gave Mentlana's shoulder a squeeze, the scars on his hand vivid against his skin because of the cold.

"It'll be all right, Mentlana. You'll see." Quinn turned and gave Charlotte a serious look, which conveyed his concern, and her heart sank.

"Walk with me back to the clinic, Charlotte." Quinn left Mentlana's bedroom.

"Of course." Charlotte packed up her things and bent down, giving Mentlana a quick kiss.

"Give him a chance, Charlotte. He didn't come up here because of me," Mentlana whispered.

Charlotte didn't answer. Instead, she left the room in silence and then slipped on her coat, following Quinn outside. The crunching of the snow under their boots was the only sound that penetrated the uneasy tension between them.

"What's your assessment?" she asked finally.

"I think it's progressed, but I won't know how much until I do an ultrasound." He opened the clinic door, holding it open for her.

"And her blood pressure… Do you think that's cause for concern?"

"We'll run a urinalysis on her when she's here." He slipped out of his coat and then helped her with hers. "Like I said to Mentlana, it'll be okay."

"How do you know that?"

"Faith?" Quinn smiled. "You said you trusted me. That meant a lot, so I hope you trust me when I say it'll be okay."

"I do," Charlotte said, and touched his arm. She did trust him, but as for everything else she wasn't sure. She moved it away from him. "I'll go get the ultrasound ready."

"Sounds good. I'll wait here to help Genen and Mentlana."

"Okay." Charlotte turned and walked down the hall away from Quinn. She was taking the coward's way out, running away from the reality that she'd played a large part in the demise in their relationship, that she may have left him long before he'd left her.

CHAPTER THIRTEEN

JUST WHEN QUINN thought he was making some headway with Charlotte she pulled away from him again. Something else had transpired at Mentlana's, but he wasn't sure what. The ultrasound had been tense, but the baby's CCAM hadn't progressed much. It wouldn't be too much longer before they'd have to fly Mentlana to Iqaluit.

Quinn helped Genen take Mentlana home and get her settled. When he returned to the clinic, Charlotte was locked away in her office, working on files, and he didn't want to disturb her, though he should. He wanted to know what was bothering her, but he also didn't want to push her away.

Instead, he pulled out his camera. First he uploaded all the pictures on his memory card to his computer and then backed up the photographs on his USB stick. Once his memory card was free of the camera, he sat down at Charlotte's kitchen table and took apart the telephoto lens to clean it out. When he'd been out ice fishing, some salt water had got into the lens so the camera's automatic zoom was not working right. The last thing he wanted was his expensive photographic equipment to get ruined.

It was the first thing he'd bought when the bandages had come off and he'd gained a bit of strength back in his hand. He loved photography, but had never able to indulge in it.

When he'd been a kid he'd wanted to be a photographer

for *National Geographic*, but when he'd announced that to his father his subscription to that magazine had ended, to be replaced by a medical journal.

Great magazine subscription for a kid of fourteen.

Quinn snorted and shook the thought of his father out of his head. There was no place for him there. Instead, he focused on the task at hand. It was delicate work, but he didn't mind it in the least. His hand hadn't been bothering him and he was able to keep a steady grip on his tools as he took apart the lens and began to clean it.

"I hope that won't void the warranty."

Quinn glanced up to see Charlotte hovering in the connecting door between her clinic and her home. She leaned against the doorjamb, watching him in fascination. The invisible wall she had put up only a couple of hours ago seemed to be down once more.

"The warranty was voided long ago." Quinn continued with his work. This time she'd have to come to him. He held his breath, waiting, and then he heard her soft footfalls as she crossed the distance between the door and the kitchen table.

"That looks like pretty intricate work. You sure you know what you're doing?"

"You doubt my mad skills?" Quinn wiped the dried salt from around the rim. "There. That should do it."

"How did you get salt into your lens?"

"I was snapping some pictures out on the ice today."

Charlotte smiled and tucked her hair behind her ear. "You weren't fishing."

"No. I hate fishing. I was there for the scenery." Quinn put his telephoto lens back together. "That was actually something my father enjoyed. He liked fishing and made me go all the time. I never caught anything, much to his chagrin."

"What do you think of the scenery up here? I mean, you weren't too interested in seeing the sights in Yellowknife."

Quinn met her gaze. "That was a different time. I was a different person."

She didn't say anything for a few moments. "I want to show you something, as you're so interested in scenery."

"I'm intrigued."

"It's outside, in the cold." Charlotte stood up.

"I'm game, but we better hurry before the sun sets."

"That's the point." She hurried into the clinic and returned with their parkas. She tossed him his and Quinn caught it.

"If it's just a sunset, I've seen many."

Charlotte grinned. "Not like this." She zipped up her parka.

"If you say so." Quinn pulled on his parka. "Lead the way."

They headed outside, towards the water. The sun was setting, and it was so low that it seemed to be touching the horizon. Being so far north, the sun looked larger in the sky. As it set behind a cloud bank, it seemed like two other small suns peeked through the clouds, giving the illusion that three suns were setting on the water.

"Wow." Quinn raised his camera and took a shot. "That *is* amazing."

Charlotte nodded. "It is. They're called sun dogs."

Quinn glanced at her. The last rays of light touched her red hair, making it seem like it was aflame. He snapped a quick picture of her, looking out over the water.

"Hey, I didn't say you could take one of me," Charlotte protested.

"I was just admiring the view."

A pink blush tinged Charlotte's skin. He slung his camera over his shoulder and moved towards her, running his hand against her cold cheek.

"Quinn, please… I'm not sure."

"You trust me, Charlotte?"

"I said I did."

"Then tell me what's wrong."

Charlotte bit her lip. "It's nothing about you. It's me this time."

Quinn was confused. "I don't understand."

"I don't, either." Charlotte sighed. The wall was up once more and he knew he couldn't press her. "It's getting dark. We need to get back to the clinic."

"Sure."

They walked in silence back to the clinic, but as they clambered over a snow bank Charlotte let out a cry of horror at what was on the other side.

Anernerk was huddled in the snow, unmoving and with no jacket.

"Oh, my God." Charlotte scrambled down quickly. "Anernerk. Oh, God. No."

Quinn was by their side in a moment. He whipped off his parka and wrapped it around the old woman. "She's breathing, but barely." He picked her up in his arms. The cold was biting at his skin, but he didn't care. This was Charlotte's family, and he cared about Anernerk, too.

Charlotte ran ahead and held open the clinic door. Quinn rushed her inside, following in the wake of Charlotte, who was preparing a nearby exam room.

Anernerk's breathing was harsh. There was a rattle in her chest.

"Set her down here," Charlotte said, placing his camera on the counter. Quinn hadn't even known he'd dropped it or that Charlotte had picked it up. The moment he'd heard Charlotte cry out, he hadn't thought about anything else except helping Anernerk.

Quinn laid the old lady down on the bed. "She can't breathe well. I'm going to have to intubate her."

"I'll get an intubation kit." Charlotte disappeared from the room.

"It'll be okay," Quinn whispered, brushing back hair from

Anernerk's forehead. Anernerk reached out and grabbed his arms, gripping him tightly with a surprising surge of strength.

"No," she said in a barely audible whisper. "No."

Quinn moved closer to her. "Anernerk, we have to."

A small smile tugged at the corner of her lips. "Don't be obstinate, Quinn Devlyn. Let me go."

Anernerk's breathing became shallower, her skin was waxy and the rattle in her chest became louder. The same sound many patients took when they were taking their final breaths.

"I have the intubation kit!" Charlotte rushed back into the room.

"She wants to go. She doesn't want intubation. It's her time."

"She can't breathe," Charlotte said, flustered and annoyed. "Goddammit, Quinn. We have to intubate her."

"No," Anernerk said. "I told him not to."

Charlotte paled. "What? Anernerk, I don't—"

"It's my time to go, Charlotte. You're a wonderful doctor, as is Dr. Devlyn, but it's my time to pass. The spirits have spoken to me."

Tears welled up in Charlotte's eyes as she leaned over Anernerk. "I can't let you go. You're all I have. You took care of me when my father died. I can't lose you."

"You have Dr. Devlyn." Anernerk reached out and stroked Charlotte's face. "I shall miss you, daughter."

"No," Charlotte cried as she gripped Anernerk's shoulders. "No, I won't let you go."

"Don't be the obstinate man's wife with dark thoughts, my child. You have to let those fears go."

Quinn held on to Charlotte's shoulders, trying to pull her away, but she shrugged him off roughly and laid out the intubation instruments.

"No," Charlotte shouted, to no one in particular. "We have to intubate."

Anernerk stretched her body and took one last breath. Her

chest stopped moving. A breeze entered the exam room and Quinn swore he could feel the old woman's soul pass through him, if he believed in that sort of thing. Which he didn't. But in this moment of Anernerk's death, he wasn't so sure.

"Time of death—sixteen-forty." Charlotte slammed the intubation tray and pushed past him, leaving the room. He heard the distant slam of her office door.

Quinn scrubbed his hand over his face and then closed Anernerk's eyes and covered her body with a sheet. He cleaned up and washed his hands, giving Charlotte her privacy as she grieved.

Twenty minutes later the door to the clinic opened and George entered the exam room. His face was broken and pale when his gaze landed on Anernerk's body.

"Charley called me. I've come to take her to the special building we have. We store the bodies out there until we can bury them."

"Of course. By all means." Quinn stepped to one side. "Do you need help?"

George shook his head. "Thanks, but no. It's Charley I'm worried about, Doc. Even though they bickered, like when you saw them, it was Grandma who reached out and healed Charlotte when she came back from Yellowknife, her and my sister. Just like when Charley's dad died, Grandma was there because Charley didn't have anyone else."

There was a bitter taste in Quinn's mouth.

He'd been the cause of her need to heal on her return from Yellowknife. He'd left her alone. It'd been his fault.

"I'll take care of Charlotte." Quinn left the exam room and headed straight for Charlotte's office, but she wasn't there.

The door to her apartment was slightly ajar and he peeked inside. She was curled up on the couch, staring blankly at the wall. She'd changed out of her heavy sweater into a T-shirt and yoga pants, her hair loose over her shoulders and a blanket lying over her hips.

When she looked at him a shudder ran down his spine. It was the same expression she'd given him when she'd been in the hospital in Yellowknife. All that was missing from the scene was the antiseptic smell of the hospital and an IV pumping blood into her veins.

Why had he walked away from her then? He'd been such a fool, but after he'd told her about New York she'd told him to go and had refused to see him. Even though they'd been engaged, they hadn't been legally family and the hospital had had to respect her wishes. He'd remained at a distance, making sure her discharge from the hospital had gone well, although she hadn't known he'd been there. And then he'd left.

It pained him that she'd shut him out of her life.

"Charlotte, I'm so sorry for your loss."

"I should've intubated her."

"She didn't want it."

Charlotte's gaze narrowed. "It doesn't matter. If I'd intubated her she'd still be alive."

Quinn moved toward her. "Be reasonable. Anernerk was a hundred and one. It was her time to go."

"No," Charlotte shouted, jumping up to face him. "They're my family. Mine. They're all I have…"

Charlotte's anger dissipated and she sat back down on the couch in defeat. She was taking out her grief on him. He didn't deserve it. He'd only been listening to the patient's wishes, whereas she had only been thinking about herself. She had let her emotions rule her. Quinn was right.

She had a tendency to be over-emotional at times. She was so used to bottling up her feelings that after a time they would erupt out of her like putting a mint in diet soda.

She was being unreasonable.

The cushion next to her dipped as Quinn sat beside her. He took her hand in his broken one. It was strong and didn't tremble.

"I'm so sorry for snapping at you, Quinn."

She leaned over and buried her face in his neck, drinking in his scent, his warmth and his strength. Strength she needed now more than ever.

Right now she needed to feel something besides pain. What she needed was physical contact with him. Even though she'd promised herself she wouldn't let him in, at this moment she wanted to drown her sorrows in him. For so long she'd been anesthetized to life and she hadn't even realized it until this moment.

Making love with Quinn would remind her she was still alive.

"Charlotte," Quinn whispered, causing goose bumps to spread across her skin. Her nipples tightened under her shirt. She pressed her body to his, trying to close off any space that remained between them.

Charlotte wanted nothing to separate them. Not at this moment.

"What can I do for you, Charlotte?" He kissed the top of her head gently as he cradled her. "I'll do anything."

"Make love to me, Quinn."

A moan escaped past his lips and his hot breath fanned her neck. "Are you sure?"

Her answer was to simply wrap her arms around his neck and run her fingers through his hair, bringing his lips to her mouth. "Yes. Make the hurt go away. Please. I need you."

No more words were needed in that moment. Her plea was silenced by a searing kiss that made her melt into him. Charlotte didn't want to let him go. As the kiss deepened he pressed her against the cushions of the couch.

"Not here," she said, reluctantly breaking off the kiss.

Quinn scooped her up in his arms, without breaking the connection of their lips as he kissed her again. He carried her the short distance down the hall to her bedroom. Her blood thundered in her ears as she thought about what was going to happen and about how much she wanted it.

He set her down and she gripped the collar of his shirt while his hands roved over her back. Quinn's pulse raced under her fingertips as she undid the buttons at the base of his throat. "I want you, Quinn."

I've never stopped wanting you.

The air seemed to crackle with almost tangible tension. It was like her first time all over again and it was only fitting. Quinn had been her first and only.

"I want you, Charlotte, but only if you're sure. You've been through so much today."

"I want this. Please."

He seemed to hesitate, but only for a moment. "I can't resist you. I've never been able to." His lips captured hers in a kiss, his tongue twining with hers. Charlotte pulled him down onto the bed, until she was kneeling in front of him. His eyes sparkled in the dim room. "I've missed you, Charlotte. God, how I've missed you."

"Me, too," she whispered. She slipped off her shoes and they clattered to the floor. Reaching for him, she dragged him into another kiss. His hands slipped down her back, the heat of his skin searing her flesh through her thin cotton shirt, making her body ache with desire. Quinn removed her shirt and then his hands moved to her back to undo the clips of her bra. He undid each one painstakingly slowly, before he slipped the straps off her shoulders.

The sharp intake of breath from Quinn when his gaze alighted on her state of half undress sent a zing of desire racing through her veins. He kissed her again, his hands moving to cup her breasts and knead them. Charlotte closed her eyes and a moan escaped at the feel of his rough caresses on her sensitized skin.

She untucked his shirt from his pants then attacked the buttons and peeled it off, tossing it over her shoulder. She ran her hands over his smooth, bare chest, before letting her fingers trail down to the waist of his trousers. He grabbed her wrists and held her there, then pushed her down roughly on the bed, pinning her as he leaned over her. He released her hands and pressed his body against hers, kissing her fervently, as though he were a condemned man, yet there was tenderness there, too.

Charlotte had missed this.

She kissed him again, snaking her arms around his neck, letting his tongue plunder her mouth, her body coming alive as if it had been in a deep sleep.

He broke the kiss and removed her yoga pants, his fingers running over her calves. Each time his fingers skimmed her flesh her body ignited, and when his thumbs slid under the side of her panties to tug them down she went up in flames. Now she was totally naked and vulnerable to him.

Quinn stood and she watched him remove his pants. Moonlight filtered through the slatted blinds. He was glorious as he bared his well-honed body to her. She remembered every exquisite inch of him. She helped him roll on a condom.

When he returned to the bed he trailed his hand over her body, lingering on her breasts. Pleasure coursed through her at his touch. He pressed his lips against one of her breasts, laving her nipple with his hot tongue. She arched her back, wanting more.

"I love making you feel this way," he said huskily.

I love it when you make me feel this way. Only she didn't say the words out loud. His hand moved down her body, between her legs. He began to stroke her, making her wet with need.

All she could think about was him replacing his hand with his mouth. The thought of where he was, what he was going to do, made her moan.

As if reading her mind, Quinn ran his tongue over her body, kissing and nipping over her stomach and hips to where he'd just been caressing. His breath against her inner thighs made her smolder and when his tongue licked between the folds of her sex, she cried out.

Instinctively she began to grind her hips upwards, her fingers slipping into his hair, holding him in place. She didn't want him to stop. Warmth spread through her body like she'd imbibed too much wine, her body taut as ecstasy enveloped her in a warm cocoon.

She was so close to the edge, but she didn't want to topple over. When she came she wanted him to be buried inside her.

Quinn shifted position and the tip of his shaft pressed against her folds. She wanted him to take her, to be his and his alone.

Even if only for this stolen time.

He thrust quickly, filling her completely. There was a small sputtering of pain, just like their first time. She clutched his shoulders as he held still, stretching her. He was buried so deep inside her.

"I'm sorry, darling," he moaned, his eyes closed. "God, you're tight. It's been far too long." He surged forward, bracing his weight on his good arm while his bad hand held her hip. She met every one of his sure thrusts.

"So tight," he murmured again.

Quinn moved harder, faster. A coil of heat unfurled deep within her. She arched her back as pleasure overtook her, the muscles of her sheath tightening around him as she came. Quinn stiffened, and spilled his seed.

He slipped out of her, falling beside her on the bed and collecting her up against him. She let him and laid her head against his damp chest, listening to his rapid breathing.

What am I doing? What have I done?

She knew exactly what she'd done. She was angry at herself for being weak and for possibly hurting them both again.

CHAPTER FOURTEEN

SHE WAS BEING watched.

Charlotte could feel Quinn's gaze boring into her back. It made her feel uneasy. Why had she slept with him again? What had she been thinking?

That was a foolish question. She knew exactly what she'd been thinking and she was now regretting it wholeheartedly in the pale light of morning. Though she had to admit she'd liked being in his arms again. Every touch, every kiss had been like a dream come true, one she hadn't woken up from when the best part had come.

Grief had pushed her carefully guarded emotions over the edge and her walls had come tumbling down.

I'm an idiot.

Charlotte glanced over her shoulder. Quinn smiled lazily at her.

"What're you looking at?" she asked.

"I just like watching you." He propped himself on his elbow. "Where are you going?"

Her stomach twisted as she thought of that little building on the edge of town and she turned her back to him again. "To see Anernerk." She stared down at her knees and tried to keep back the tears threatening to spill.

The mattress dipped and Quinn scooted towards her. "Do you think that's wise?"

"Wise or not, I thought of her as a mother. She raised me as her own and it's my duty to be there." Besides, she had to put some distance between her and Quinn. Last night had been wonderful, but it needed to end there.

"A tradition?"

"Yes." A sigh escaped. She was not relishing her duty because she didn't want to face the reality that Anernerk was gone. Someone else she loved who'd left her.

You have Quinn. All you have to do is reach out and grab him.

Did she have Quinn? He hadn't said anything to the contrary. She might trust him for his surgical abilities, but she didn't trust handing her heart over to him again. Charlotte didn't want to pin all her hope on the notion that he *might* stay. She wasn't sure if he truly understood why it meant so much for her to stay up here and devote her life of medicine to these far-flung communities.

And she couldn't ask him to stay with her, giving up the life he wanted. Neither would she hold it against him this time when he left.

"I understand. I'm just worried about your emotional state."

Charlotte stood, but wouldn't look at him. She wasn't brave enough to meet his gaze, to let him have all of her.

"My emotional state is fine." Then she met his gaze and saw tenderness, concern and perhaps something more in his eyes.

Walk away, Charlotte.

"I have to go."

"Will you be back soon?" he asked.

"Does it matter?"

"It does. I want to talk about going to Iqaluit."

Charlotte took a step back, shocked. Did he want to work in Iqaluit? She hoped she hadn't led him on. "Why?"

"Unless you have laparoscopic equipment up here, I need to get to a facility that does. We're going to do a dry run of Mentlana's procedure in a skills lab."

Her heart sank in disappointment. *What were you expecting? Really.* "Yes, well, I don't... I mean, I'll have to file a flight plan."

"Then file one. We need to get down there as soon as we can."

"You want me to come with you?"

Quinn raised an eyebrow. "How else are you going to assist me?"

"Assist you? I thought you were joking before."

"I don't joke about surgery."

"I'm flattered, but I can't go to Iqaluit with you."

Quinn frowned. "I thought you still had a surgical license."

"I do. I can still perform some surgery, but I can't leave Cape Recluse."

"Why not?"

"I'm the only physician here."

"And your only current high-risk patient is Mentlana?"

"Yes."

"Then what choice do you have? You need to go through a dry run with me in a skills lab. You fly, George flies and it's a two-hour flight, so you won't be separated from your patients up here. You can spend a few days in Iqaluit with me, practicing. This is for your best friend, Charlotte."

Damn. Quinn was right.

"I'll talk to George. We'll arrange something, but after Anernerk's funeral."

"Deal."

She turned to leave then spun back round. "You're serious? You want me to assist?"

"Positive." He lay back against the pillows. "Only you."

Only me?

It gave her pleasure to know that he did trust her, that he had faith in her abilities to assist him, a renowned neonatal surgeon.

Of course she'd be an idiot to pass up this opportunity.

She'd file the flight plan with the airfield as soon as she was able to. Right now she had to focus on Anernerk and it was going to be hard. Even thinking about Anernerk laid out, waiting until they could dig through the permafrost, made her throat constrict. They'd have a memorial in a day or so and then bury her when the ground was softer.

Charlotte slipped on her parka at the door and headed out into the cold, but winter's bite didn't have any effect on her. Her mind was whirring with several things, Anernerk, Mentlana, the baby and, of course, Quinn.

Charlotte paused in front of the little cabin and took a deep, steadying breath.

I can do this. Anernerk wanted me here. She wanted me to be a part of this moment.

The handle to the door shook in her gloved hands as she opened it and stepped inside. The local ladies, including Lucy and Lorna, had placed Anernerk's body on one of the hides Anernerk's father had cured—a caribou which had been special to the old woman.

Charlotte stepped forward without saying anything. She'd seen this ritual performed before and she'd taken part in it as well. This time, however, it was much more personal. She took the wet rag Lorna handed her and gingerly picked up Anernerk's arm. She began to wash Anernerk's paper-thin skin.

A draft rushed at her back. Charlotte turned as Mentlana lumbered into the room. Two steps and Charlotte was by her side.

"Is everything okay?"

"I'm all right," Mentlana chided.

"You shouldn't be out of bed." Charlotte gripped her shoulder. "Don't you understand what bed rest is?"

Mentlana snorted. "Please. Genen already gave me that lecture. He brought me over on the dogsled, tied to the back of his snowmobile."

"What?" Charlotte was going to have a stern talking to Genen.

"He went like five kilometers an hour. Besides, it was my idea."

"Apparently, pregnancy has rendered you into a lunatic."

Mentlana sighed. "I wanted to be here. Let me braid her hair. I'll just do that and go back home."

"Okay. But then Genen's taking you home."

Mentlana nodded. "Thanks, Charley." She moved slowly to Anernerk's head and began to brush out the snowy white hair.

They finished preparing Anernerk's body. Mentlana braided the hair beautifully and was taken back home by Genen. The elders dressed Anernerk in traditional clothing and then wrapped her body in the caribou hide on which she'd been laid out.

Charlotte stood back, tears blurring her vision, but they didn't escape. She watched the final rituals. Later there would be requiems for Anernerk and her life.

There was nothing more she could do here. It was at times like this Charlotte felt helpless, useless. She was a healer and death was a blow to her. She'd lost and death had won.

"Can I have a moment alone with her?"

The other women nodded and exited the cabin. The sound of the door shutting behind her thundered in her head like a deafening blow of finality. She was alone with Anernerk, the outside world closed out so she could say her private farewells.

Charlotte would have to be quick. It was too cold outside for the other women to be out there long. She took a step toward Anernerk, the woman who had kept her from being lost in the system as an orphan. The woman who'd encouraged and nourished her dreams. The only mother Charlotte had known. She brushed her fingers across Anernerk's cold cheek.

"Aanak," she whispered. "I love you. You saved my life. I don't know how I'll go on without you, but I know you would want me to and I will. I hope you have the peace you were looking for." Tears rolled down Charlotte's face and she brushed them away.

"May the spirits guide you home." Charlotte opened the door and the elders returned to finish the preparations. She nodded to one of the elders and slipped out of the cabin. The sun was beginning to set and the stiffness in her shoulder alerted her to the fact she'd been tending to Anernerk's body for some time.

The lights from her house flooded out on the snow and a warm sensation built in the pit of her stomach. Quinn was there, waiting for her. She didn't have to be alone tonight if she was willing to take the risk and be with him again.

That was not a risk she was willing to take. She wouldn't lead him on.

Too much water had passed under the bridge and Charlotte couldn't see a way back to reclaim what they'd had. She wouldn't lose her heart to him again.

When she entered her home the scent of garlic hung heavily in the air and her stomach rumbled in response. Her home smelled like an Italian eatery, which was odd. Nothing in town was open. Today was a day of mourning for Anernerk. When someone died, communities became ghost towns for a couple of days.

Charlotte hung her jacket on the hook by the door and peered into the kitchen. The windows were steamed up and Quinn was moving back and forth between the stove and the table.

She suppressed a chuckle when she spied the old frilly apron, which had been her mother's, wrapped around his waist. She'd kept it for purely sentimental reasons, but seeing Quinn in it, tearing around the kitchen, amused her.

On the table was a clean white lace tablecloth, and two emergency candles were alight in a couple of old pickle jars. Two glass tumblers were filled with grape juice. It was the most romantic thing he'd ever done for her.

Damn. What is he doing?

Quinn cursed as he lifted the lid on a steaming pot. He shook his hand and stuck his finger in his mouth.

"There's some aloe vera in the living room. That's best for burns."

He spun round. "You're back. I wasn't sure when you were going to come back."

"Neither was I." She took a cautious step into the kitchen. "What're you doing? I didn't think you could cook."

"I can cook one thing. Garlic bread. But I felt I needed to feed you more than that." He gestured to the bubbling pots on the stovetop. "I found some spaghetti and sauce in the cupboards. Not much fresh stuff."

"Fresh stuff is hard to come by and very expensive."

Quinn sighed. "It's pretty bad when the town's doctor can't even afford some button mushrooms."

Charlotte chuckled and picked up a spoon, stirring the clumps of spaghetti before it was too late to be saved. "There's some canned mushrooms in the cupboard."

"Sacrilegious," he teased, but he pulled out the can and opened it, draining the juice into the sink before rinsing the mushrooms off. "Oh, look at that, they're even sliced."

"Extra fancy," she teased.

"But essential for this dinner."

"Oh?" Charlotte was intrigued. "Why essential?"

"I'm trying to replicate the meal we had in Niagara Falls on our first spring break away from medical school." Quinn dumped the mushrooms in the sauce.

The first time they'd made love. She remembered. They'd stayed in a cheap motel on the Canadian side of the falls and had got two coupons for dinner at an Italian restaurant.

The last thing she needed tonight was to be reminded of that moment.

"Quinn, this isn't necessary."

"Let me do this for you, Charlotte. You're tired and grieving."

Charlotte sighed in resignation. There was no harm in letting him make dinner. They'd been sharing meals since he'd arrived and they had been innocent enough.

"Hey, bring that pasta here. The sauce is ready."

"Sure." Charlotte dumped the spaghetti back into the pot and placed it on a cool range.

"Go sit down. I'll be serving you tonight." Quinn pushed her towards the table and she didn't fight him. She sat down and waited for him to serve dinner. The garlic bread smelled heavenly and she couldn't remember the last time someone had made her a spaghetti dinner. Hell, she couldn't even recall the last time she'd eaten spaghetti. When she cooked for herself, when she allowed herself time to eat, it was fast and quick. She worried, briefly, how long the ingredients had been in her pantry.

It wouldn't matter. Quinn had tried and she was going to eat the meal, though she might regret it later. The way she was feeling now, she could eat a whole plate of muktuk if given half the chance.

"Voilà." Quinn set the plate down in front of her. A huge mound of spaghetti with Bolognese sauce and a crispy side of cheesy garlic bread made her stomach growl loudly in appreciation.

"The first taste is with the eyes."

"Is that your subtle way of telling me it won't taste good?" she asked.

He winked. "Taste is all in the mind."

"Oh, dear." She grinned.

Quinn picked up his tumbler of juice. "To Anernerk and the wonderful century she graced this earth."

"To Anernerk." The words were hard to get out and it was even harder to swallow the juice. She set down the tumbler and Quinn's hand slid across the table, his fingers twining with hers. She pulled her hand away.

"I'm sorry. I can't." She couldn't let him touch her. She was too weak.

"It's okay. You're mourning. You have every right to mourn her. You loved her."

"Thank you for understanding. I need my space."

"I went through my own situation not that long ago."

"Your father. Of course. I'm sorry."

Quinn shrugged. "Don't be. He wasn't the most loving of fathers."

"You never really told me how your parents felt about me."

"I know." Quinn didn't meet her gaze.

"That bad, huh?"

He grinned. "He wanted me to marry a socialite, or whatever Toronto's equivalent is to that. Marrying the daughter of some 'hippy'—even if she was a physician—wasn't good enough."

"My father was a doctor. He was far from being a hippy."

"You weren't my father's ideal idea of a wife for me."

"Apparently not for you, either." She regretted the words instantly.

Quinn's smiled faded and he took a bite of his spaghetti. "I could say the same in reverse."

Guilt washed over her. "You could."

They ate in silence, but it was hard to chew. The food was like sawdust in her mouth.

"My cooking is that bad, then?" Quinn asked, breaking the tension.

She glanced up and the earlier twinkle was back in Quinn's eyes. "It's great—better than those brownies."

He groaned. "Let's not bring that up again. Please tell me I'm improving."

Charlotte picked up a piece of garlic bread and took a bite. It was like pure heaven, compared to the clumpy mess that was the spaghetti. The garlic bread melted in her mouth like cheesy goodness. She could marry the garlic bread and she would if it asked her.

"I take it from your orgasmic expression that I did quite well with the bread."

"You did," she said between bites. "You're right."

"About what?"

"You can cook garlic bread. It's divine." She took another bite. "Of course, it could be because I haven't had *real* garlic bread in about three years and I'm desperate for it."

They ate the rest of the meal. She'd forgotten how delicious someone else's cooking was, even if it was Quinn's.

"What do you think?" he asked, as he poured another glass of juice.

"Could be better." She grinned and then winked.

"Better? I ought to take you over my knee and spank you for that remark."

Quinn's jest instantly sobered her up. She set down her fork and then picked up her plate, taking it to the sink.

"Did I say something wrong, Charlotte?" he asked.

"No. Nothing." It was all becoming too easy with Quinn again. He was charismatic and broke through her defenses so easily. "I'm really tired. I need to go to bed."

"Okay. I'll clean up," he said.

Charlotte nodded and without so much as a look she retreated to the safety of her bedroom, locking the door behind her. The bed was still messy and Quinn's scent still lingered in the air, causing heat to creep up her neck. The memory of last night's kisses were suddenly fresh in her brain once more.

She wanted him still, but she wouldn't give in.

Instead, she stripped her bed of the sheets and shoved them in the laundry hamper, shutting the lid firmly.

For her own sanity, she had to stick to her original plan and keep her heart on ice.

CHAPTER FIFTEEN

AFTER ANERNERK'S MEMORIAL, Quinn and Charlotte moved down to Iqaluit. Quinn's reputation as a surgeon had preceded him and the hospital was willing to bend over backwards to accommodate them. He knew the hospital was trying to woo him into staying permanently.

For a month Charlotte traveled between Cape Recluse and Iqaluit as they prepared for Mentlana's eventual surgery.

Charlotte was polite to Quinn and willing to learn, but the barriers were back up and it smarted. Although what could he expect? The night they'd made love, Charlotte had been looking for comfort, not to renew their relationship.

And he had to respect her wishes, even though he wished the reverse. Once Mentlana successfully delivered he would return to Toronto and she'd remain here.

You could stay.

Only what would be the use of staying if Charlotte didn't want him?

There were times Quinn thought she was pulling away, distancing herself from him, building those walls back up. Then at other times it was like the years hadn't passed them and their separation had never happened.

"That's it, keep the needle steady." Quinn watched the monitor as Charlotte manipulated the laparoscope in the lab. She was doing quite well. They'd done a couple of dry runs for placing a thoracoamniotic shunt, the most minimally invasive treatment for Mentlana's baby.

Quinn began to teach Charlotte everything he knew. Charlotte kept in close contact with George, who flew in once a week to take Charlotte back to check up on Mentlana and her other patients. No one else was seriously ill or needed the kind of care Mentlana did.

The residents of Cape Recluse understood what Doc Charley was doing and they didn't mind. The community was still shaken by Anernerk's death and everyone was rooting for this baby. Cape Recluse needed a happy event. This baby represented the hope of a small community.

When he'd last checked on Mentlana, her baby's CCAM was still within the safe range and wasn't pressing on the heart yet. "Yet" was the operative word. At any moment the CCAM could worsen. He was holding off operating, hoping to get her further along in her pregnancy.

The pressure to succeed was keenly felt. Mentlana was thirty weeks, now, but if he could get her to thirty-five then the baby had a better chance of survival should he have to deliver him early.

Quinn wasn't a praying man, but he was wishing for that right now with all his heart. He didn't want to have to perform an in utero procedure. The pediatric specialist in Iqaluit would be quite capable of handling Mentlana's baby and the CCAM if delivered after thirty-five weeks.

It was the surgery that had the young specialist apprehensive. Dr. Richards, the pediatrician there, hadn't done many. Indeed she spent as much time in the skills lab as Charlotte.

Plans were being put in place with the obstetrician, as well. Everything seemed to be running smoothly. However, when Charlotte had returned from her last stint in Cape Recluse three days ago, she'd seemed out of sorts.

She'd been aloof since the dinner he'd made her, but now

she looked drawn, tired and ill. He hoped she wasn't catching a cold. If she got sick, she couldn't be allowed near the O.R.

"Dr. Devlyn?" Charlotte said, disturbing his silent rumination. She'd taken to addressing him in a professional manner in front of the other surgeons.

"Good. Now place the shunt. Do you remember how?"

"I do."

Even though they weren't practicing on living tissue, there was a certain finesse about placing such a small shunt inside something so tiny and fragile.

"Then let's see."

Charlotte bit her lip, her brow furrowing as she concentrated and placed it.

"Good." Quinn let out an inward sigh of relief, his shoulders relaxing. Charlotte hadn't managed it yesterday, but each day, she was improving. His hope was that she could perform the surgery with Dr. Richards, should his hand fail. He rubbed the appendage in question. It'd been paining him after too many hours in the lab, and the thought of it not being strong enough to operate worried him.

"Excellent job, Dr. James," praised Dr. Richards, who was taking copious notes in a flipbook.

Charlotte took a deep breath and smiled. "Thank you, Dr. Richards. Now, I'd better head back to the hotel and pack. George should be here soon for my trip back to Cape Recluse."

"Of course," Quinn said. He would miss her. He always did when she returned to Cape Recluse.

"I'll call you about Mentlana's status when I examine her later today."

"Thank you, Dr. James. I look forward to your assessment."

Charlotte left the skills lab while Quinn cursed inwardly.

You're being selfish, Quinn Devlyn. Tell her you miss her. But he couldn't. Even though he didn't want to be parted from her and wanted to heal the rift between them, he wasn't sure if he wanted to spend the rest of his life in Nunavut in the cold and ice.

The selfish side of him wondered if she'd come to Toronto to be with him, but he doubted that very much. She hadn't left the North five years ago when they'd been engaged, so why would she now?

This was where Charlotte belonged. But he wasn't sure if he did.

He turned to Dr. Richards. "I'd better be off. I have some sonograms to review." Quinn excused himself from the lab, relieved he didn't have to talk shop with Dr. Richards, who usually talked his ear off. Right now his head was pounding behind his eyes.

When he was in the locker room he pulled off his scrubs and deposited them in the laundry receptacle before washing his hands. As soon as the water hit his skin the muscles in his palm tensed, forcing his fingers to curl upwards, freezing in a clawlike position.

"Dammit," he cursed as he gripped his bad hand with his good one. He massaged the palm, willing the spasms to cease before someone walked in on him. His whole arm was tense, the muscles rigid up past the elbow. It'd been a long time since he'd had a spasm like this, where it locked his entire arm into a useless tangle of sinew and flesh.

How the hell could he even contemplate operating on Mentlana? This just proved all his fears. There was no way he could risk doing a delicate surgery such as a thoracoamniotic shunt or fetal resection when his muscle spasms were so unpredictable.

Bile rose in his throat as he thought about holding such a delicate, fragile life in his hands and having a spasm like this. He would crush the fetus.

His muscles began to relax under his ministrations. Once his arm ceased tensing up he was able to relax his fingers.

Quinn's other hand ached from massaging his damaged one so long and so hard.

Dammit.

His phone buzzed and he pulled it out of his trouser pocket. It was a text from Charlotte, who needed to speak to him before she left for Cape Recluse. He didn't want her to see him like this. He texted back that he had been held up at the hospital and then jammed his phone back in his pocket.

Quinn pulled his arm close to his side, cradling it as pins and needles coursed up and down from his elbow to the tips of his fingers. The aftermath of the spasm always felt like he'd fallen asleep on his hand. He had to leave the hospital before anyone saw his hand all clenched and tense, before anyone suspected anything. He quickly dressed in his street clothes, his hand impeding the process slightly.

How the hell was he going to tell Charlotte he couldn't do the surgery?

Right now he needed some liquid courage, but he didn't know where he was going to find it in Iqaluit and he didn't relish the idea of wandering through bitterly cold streets in an attempt to do so.

"Ah, Dr. Devlyn. Just the man I was looking for."

Quinn groaned inwardly as the chief surgeon approached him, followed by members of the board of directors. He'd nothing against Dr. Spicer or the board—in fact, he was grateful they were willing to open up their hospital and allow him to be here when their hospital was full of surgeons—but he didn't want to be stopped at the moment.

He didn't want them to see him this way.

Dr. Spicer stopped in front of Quinn and the board members closed in around him. He was trapped, his escape route cut off.

Deep breath.

"Dr. Devlyn, may I introduce you to our board—Mr. Leonard Saltzman, Mrs. Jennifer Chenery and Mr. Harry Westman."

Quinn shook each member's hand, forcing out pleasantries through gritted teeth, keeping his bad hand behind his back.

"Dr. Devlyn is a renowned neonatal surgeon. He's up here preparing for surgery on a possible congenital cystic adenomatoid malformation on an Inuk woman's fetus."

"Impressive," Jennifer Chenery said, looking him up and down with an appreciative eye. "Are you carrying out the entire procedure as well as the birth?"

"No," Quinn replied. "No. Your head of obstetrics is more than capable of assisting me. He will be delivering the infant at term."

There were a few murmurs, and Quinn knew without a doubt they were impressed. He knew Mrs. Chenery was, from the way she was eyeing him like he was piece of chocolate cake or something.

"You worked at Manhattan Mercy for a time, is that correct, Dr. Devlyn?" Leonard Saltzman asked.

"Yes, I did, and then I returned to Canada. I worked at Mount Sinai for a couple of years before taking a sabbatical after my father's death."

"Dr. Devlyn is highly praised by Manhattan Mercy's chief of surgery," Dr. Spicer told the board members.

Quinn's stomach twisted and he had a feeling about where this conversation was going, but he wasn't sure if he was in a position to listen to it. Dr. Spicer was still talking him up to the board members and Quinn supposed he was talking to him as well, but Quinn couldn't hear anything but muffled words.

"Dr. Devlyn?" Dr. Spicer said.

"Sorry, Dr. Spicer. I was thinking about… I was contemplating something about a patient's procedure. Please forgive me." Quinn tried to extricate himself from the conversation, but it didn't work.

"No problem, Dr. Devlyn. I know you're a busy man. The board members were just leaving."

Quinn nodded and shook their hands as they left, until it

was only he and Dr. Spicer standing in the surprisingly quiet corridor.

"I'd best be on my way, as well," Quinn said, but Dr. Spicer reached out and grabbed his shoulder.

"A moment of your time, Dr. Devlyn."

"Yes, of course. Lead the way." Dr. Spicer opened the door to a small consult room they'd been standing in front of.

Dr. Spicer shut the door and motioned for Quinn to sit. "I think you know why I've asked you in here."

"I have an inkling."

Dr. Spicer grinned. "We want to offer you a position here in Iqaluit. We want you to head up a world-class neonatal unit. Right now we're currently flying cases like Mrs. Tikivik to Ottawa or Toronto because se don't have the facilities or surgical capabilities, but our board of directors is planning to change that. We want to provide a service like that for our community."

Quinn scrubbed his hand over his face. "Do you think the territory will fund an endeavor like this?"

Dr. nodded. "I think so and I know the communities will rally for federal support, too. We need physicians with the know-how up here. We need to provide a more extensive neonatal facility for our patients and we want you to spearhead it."

"I don't know, Dr. Spicer." Quinn, for some unknown reason, couldn't come flat out and turn Dr. Spicer down and he couldn't think of an excuse.

So what was holding him back from accepting?

The position his father had left for him in Toronto? No. He didn't care about becoming Chief of Surgery. Not really.

Dr. Spicer looked crestfallen, but smiled nonetheless. "Understandable, but the board is willing to do whatever it takes to get you, Dr. Devlyn."

"Let me think on it."

"Of course, take all the time you need, Quinn. The offer doesn't have a termination date."

"Very generous of you."

Dr. Spicer opened the consult-room door and Quinn exited, Dr. Spicer shaking his hand as he was leaving.

Why didn't I just say no? Why didn't I say yes?

Quinn couldn't figure it out. He couldn't think straight and his mind was a bit too full at the moment. All the expectations were weighing heavily on his shoulders. And then there was Charlotte.

Beautiful, wonderful, loving Charlotte, who'd let him back inside her protective walls, or so he'd thought.

"Hey, Quinn!"

Quinn glanced over his shoulder to see Dr. Patterson, the OB/GYN on Mentlana's case, approaching. He was dressed in street clothes, with a duffel bag slung over his shoulder.

"Carlisle." Quinn greeted him, as Dr. Patterson approached. "I thought you'd gone home."

"I'm on my way." Dr. Patterson looked him over from head to toe. "You look like roadkill."

"I feel like it."

Carlisle clapped him on the back. "You need a stiff drink."

"I do, but didn't know where I'd be able to find one."

"I know just the place if you care to join me."

"I would." Quinn relaxed. "Lead the way."

CHAPTER SIXTEEN

THREE DAYS AGO, when she had last been in Cape Recluse, her life had changed because a month ago she'd lost her head and had made love with Quinn. She hadn't believed the over-the-counter pregnancy test she'd used and had Rosie draw some blood.

The blood test confirmed it as well.

She was pregnant. And shocked because they'd used protection. The condom must've failed, because there was no denying it. She was already a month gone.

It thrilled and terrified her to her very core.

She wanted a family. She wanted to be a mother, but being pregnant scared her witless. What if she lost this one? It would be too much to bear.

Charlotte stuffed some clothes in her duffel bag, trying not to think about having to leave again, especially leaving Quinn again. She tried to distance herself from Quinn, to keep her walls secure, but to no avail.

She thought about him constantly. Her heart once more belonged to him, but she wasn't sure how she could tell him that. As well as tell him that she was pregnant again. The last time she'd told him they were expecting it hadn't gone well at all.

An hour ago a text had come in and she'd picked up her phone. Quinn had got her text about needing to speak with him, but he had been held up at the hospital.

She was tempted to text him and tell him why she needed to speak to him, but a text wasn't going to cut it. She needed to tell him face-to-face, even though she was afraid to risk her heart again.

Charlotte wondered if he suspected her condition. He'd been so distracted and aloof in the skills lab today and she'd been having extreme morning sickness. She could barely keep anything down and it was beginning to show in her pallor.

No, he couldn't know. She'd only just found out herself and he hadn't noticed last time she'd been pregnant.

Perhaps he was regretting his decision to allow her to assist.

Yesterday, when she had messed up and inserted that test shunt too roughly, causing the laparoscope to go deeper, thus killing the fetus, he'd come up behind her and placed his hands over hers, guiding her through another run. His gentle, firm touch was so sure and steady.

Don't be a coward.

Charlotte had to see him, couldn't go to Cape Recluse without telling him. She left her packing and was about to go track Quinn down when there was a knock at her door. Charlotte opened it and there he was, leaning against the doorjamb.

"Quinn?" Charlotte was surprised to see him. He looked a bit disheveled and there was a strong odor of beer. "Are you drunk? Where did you find alcohol?"

"Dr. Patterson is a member of the local legion."

Charlotte stepped to the side and allowed him into the room before shutting the door. "You shouldn't be drinking. Mentlana might go into distress any time now."

Quinn shook his head. "First of all, I'm not drunk. I only had pop. Someone spilled their beer on me."

"Well, that's a relief. The last thing a surgeon of your caliber needs to be doing is drinking."

Quinn snorted. "My caliber indeed," he mumbled, as he sat down on the edge of the bed.

"What's wrong? You were acting very strangely in the lab today."

He ignored her question. "Secondly, you don't need me. You're perfectly capable of doing the surgery on your own."

Charlotte paled. "What're you talking about? I'm just a GP—you're the surgeon. You've done this countless times. You know the call to make and when to make it. I'm just here to assist."

"You're not just an assistant, Charlotte. You're going to take point on Mentlana's baby."

"You are drunk." Charlotte snorted.

"Not at all."

"Then why am I suddenly taking point?"

"My hand spasmed. I don't want to risk that happening during surgery. You have to take over. I know you can do it."

The room spun. She felt dizzy. She sat down next to him on the bed. *Take point?* She was a general surgeon, not a specialist.

"I can't take point, Quinn."

"I've already talked to Dr. Patterson. He'll vouch for your ability and be overseeing you every step of the way."

Dread coursed down her spine. "And where will you be?" she asked cautiously.

"I don't know, Charlotte. Where will I be?"

The blood drained from her face. "What do you mean?" Though she knew.

"You know what I mean." He raked his fingers through his hair. "Damn it, Charlotte, I can't stay here."

Charlotte's heart skipped a beat and it felt like a great weight was pressing on her chest, stopping her from breathing. He was doing it again. He was finding some excuse and running away.

"What about Mentlana?"

Quinn cursed under his breath. "I just told you, you and Carlisle Patterson can handle it. I can't."

"I think you can."

He looked up at her, angry. "Dammit, Charlotte, my hand spasmed. If you let me near Mentlana and her baby, I might kill them."

She was opening her mouth to say something when her phone began to ring. She answered it. "Dr. James speaking."

"Doc Charley, it's George. I'm at the airport and we're transporting Mentlana to the hospital. She's gone into pre-term labor."

"I'll be right there." Charlotte snapped her phone shut. Her stomach lurched and she came precariously close to losing her lunch. There was so much more she wanted to say to Quinn, but she didn't have time to deal with him and his brooding.

Mentlana needed her.

"What's wrong?" he asked.

"What does it matter to you? You're heading back to Toronto to wallow." She tried to push past him but he grabbed her arm and spun her round.

"Charlotte, I won't risk her baby. If I do the surgery on Mentlana and she or her baby dies, you'll loathe me."

"You care how I would feel about you?"

Quinn's face relaxed. "Of course, I do. I don't want to kill the baby. I'm afraid. My hand…it clenched so hard today."

Charlotte touched his face. "You won't. I'll be with you every step of the way."

"If I'm handling the fetus… Oh, God, I don't even want to think about it." He tried to move away, but she gripped him by the shoulders.

"You can do this. I'll help you."

She held her breath, waiting for his response. Quinn nodded. "All right. And you're right. I can."

"Good. Now, we have to head to the hospital. That was George on the phone and Mentlana has gone into preterm labor."

Quinn nodded again. "I'll grab a coffee in the cafeteria.

Hopefully the on-call obstetrician is smart enough to try and stop the contractions. Let's go."

Charlotte grabbed her purse, ready to face whatever fate had to throw at them.

Charlotte was reading Mentlana's chart while Mentlana was napping. The obstetrician on call had been able to stop the contractions, so they had that going for them: the less stress on the baby the better, and a contracting uterus wasn't particularly helpful to a fetus with a CCAM.

Genen had been absolutely frantic until they'd got everything under control, then he'd crashed and was sleeping on a nearby cot while Lorna knitted in the corner. The clicking of Lorna's knitting needles mixing with the beeps and hums of the monitors in the dim room was oddly soothing to Charlotte.

She'd been on her feet for almost twenty-four hours since Mentlana had arrived. George had gone back up to Cape Recluse as they needed someone with some medical experience there.

"How's it looking, Doc?" Lorna whispered.

"She's stable. Dr. Devlyn is going to do a portable sonogram soon. He's just gone to get the machine. And then we'll assess what needs to be done."

Lorna nodded slowly. "How about you take a rest? You're in your first trimester and with your history of the previous miscarriage you need to take it easy."

Charlotte's mouth dropped open. "How did you know?"

Lorna shrugged but didn't look up from her knitting. "I've been a midwife longer than you've been alive, Charlotte James. I know when a woman is expecting." Lorna glanced up at her. "I'm thrilled for you, by the way."

"Thank you. I have to admit I'm nervous."

"You have every right to be, but I'm sure everything will be okay."

"No one can be certain of that." Charlotte sighed. "I mean,

there are so many variables, so many things that could go wrong."

Like car accidents. Look at Quinn—he'd had a terrible one that had damaged his surgical hand and only his hand. What were the odds on that?

"Yes, that's true," Lorna admitted. "But if you worry about the what-ifs, you'll make yourself sick. You're a physician. You're looking at statistics of what can go wrong all the time. But look at the number of births that go right. What happened to you was a tragedy, Charlotte, but it wasn't anything you did that caused you to lose your baby."

Charlotte nodded. "You're right."

"I know it." Lorna went back to knitting, a smug smile plastered across her face. "Your baby will be healthy, as will you, Doc Charley."

"What?" Mentlana asked groggily. "Who's pregnant?"

Charlotte pulled a rolling stool up beside Mentlana. "How are you feeling?"

"Like a beached whale, of course." Mentlana winced. "Now, who's pregnant? Dish the dirt. I may be drugged up with who knows what, but I know I heard Lorna and you talking about a pregnancy." Mentlana's eyes widened and Charlotte didn't need to tell her anything. Her friend had figured it out. "You're pregnant."

"Yes. It's me."

"Oh, my God, that's wonderful, Charley." Mentlana paused. "It's Devlyn's, right?"

Charlotte rolled her eyes. "Who else's would it be?"

"Does he know?"

"No." Charlotte's cheeks flushed. "I want to tell him but…"

"You're afraid," Mentlana offered.

Charlotte nodded. "Terrified. The last time didn't end well. He wasn't thrilled about the prospect, either."

"You need to tell him. He has the right to know." Mentlana reached out and took her hand, giving it a squeeze. "And if he wants no part of it, you'll have a baby. You'd make an excellent mother."

Charlotte smiled. "Thank you."

Mentlana grinned. "I'm so happy for you." She rubbed her belly. "You know, I always wonder about that phrase about God only giving you what you can handle. I wondered about the purpose of making me and my child so sick and putting us through this torment, but I think I know why, now."

"Mentlana, I wouldn't wish that kind of fate on anyone."

Her friend smiled. "'Oh, ye of little faith.'"

"How are we this morning?" Quinn asked as he pushed a portable sonogram into the room. Genen roused from his slumber with a groan. "Sorry, Genen," Quinn apologized, realizing he'd woken him up.

"It's okay, Doc." Genen yawned.

Quinn set up the machine but he squeezed Charlotte's shoulder as he passed. "You okay? You need your rest. You look beat."

"I'll rest after I know how Mentlana's baby is doing." Charlotte saw Mentlana's pointed look, but Charlotte kept her mouth shut as Dr. Richards walked into the room, followed by Dr. Patterson.

"Genen, Mentlana, this is Dr. Richards, a pediatric specialist, and Dr. Patterson, the head of obstetrics. They'll be helping us with your baby."

"Nice to meet you," Genen said quietly, taking a seat beside his wife.

"I'll just do a quick sonogram to see how the baby's CCAM is progressing."

"Sure thing," Mentlana agreed, but Charlotte could tell by the waver in her voice that she was nervous. It was the first sign of apprehension Mentlana had expressed in a long time. Even when they'd wheeled her into the hospital yesterday she had been pretty upbeat. Nothing seemed to faze Mentlana Tikivik.

Charlotte admired Mentlana's bravery. She reached out and
brushed Mentlana's hair back from her forehead, but when she
looked up she saw a strange expression—a cold, calculating
look—pass over Dr. Richards's face, like she was trying to
find some fault with her.

The sound of the baby's heartbeat filled the darkened room
and Charlotte forgot about Dr. Richards and watched the baby
on the screen. The lesion was growing and soon hydrops would
start. Mentlana could develop mirror syndrome. If that happened, the baby's chance of survival greatly diminished.

Charlotte's stomach twisted and she resisted the urge to
give in to the morning sickness. *Please, don't let me throw up
now.* The last thing she needed was Dr. Richards poking her
nose into why she was vomiting during a routine sonogram.

"There we go," Quinn announced. "All done." He wiped off
Mentlana's swollen belly and then sent Charlotte a quick look
which conveyed his concern, one she understood all too well.

"Well, Doc Devlyn?" Genen asked, his voice tight with
barely contained worry.

"We're going to discuss the next steps, but I'm pleased your
contractions have stopped now, Mentlana. That's very good."

Mentlana nodded and gripped Genen's hand. "Thank you,
Doctors."

Quinn escorted Dr. Patterson and Dr. Richards out of the
room. Charlotte kissed Mentlana's forehead. "I'll be back as
soon as I can with some news. Just relax, take it easy, bug the
nurses for anything you want...."

Mentlana chuckled. "Okay."

Charlotte left the room and pulled a cracker out of her
pocket. She had a sleeve of them in her lab coat. Her morning sickness was turning into all-day sickness. She had to get
a consult with Dr. Patterson soon and get some Diclectin to
keep her vomiting at bay.

When she approached the meeting room she could hear

raised voices. It was never a good sign when surgeons disagreed.

"Dr. James shouldn't be allowed to do the surgery."

Charlotte paused, hearing Dr. Richards's voice over the din. Her heart skipped a beat and then sank to the soles of her feet. Her first instinct was to back away, but Mentlana was her patient and Quinn needed her. She wasn't going to be bullied by the other surgeons. With a deep breath she pushed open the door. The arguing stopped immediately

Dr. Richards's lips were pursed in a tight thin line as their gazes locked.

"Dr. Richards." Charlotte nodded curtly. "I understand you have some problem about my involvement in this case."

"Dr. James, it's nothing," Quinn said, trying to soothe the tension in the room.

"I would love to hear everyone's opinions, Dr. Devlyn." Charlotte took a seat across from Dr. Richards. "Every surgeon's input is invaluable, especially when it involves Mentlana Tikivik."

It was a good move to pump up a young surgeon's ego. Surgeons could be silly and petty creatures that way. It was like her mother's old saying about catching more flies with honey than vinegar. Or Anernerk's saying of always treating your children with respect because they'll replace you one day, and from the way it sounded, Dr. Richards was trying to replace her in the surgical suite.

Dr. Richards was shocked. A small smile even cracked her usually serious facade. "It's not that I question your skill and value as a physician, Dr. James. I have spent a lot of time with you in the lab and am vastly impressed with your handling of instruments. You have the skills of a surgeon, but I'm concerned about your familiarity with the patient."

"What do you mean?" Charlotte asked.

"There's a reason physicians don't operate on family members, whether blood or a close bond."

"And your point?"

Dr. Richards's eyes narrowed. "I don't think you will act rationally in there. With myself, Dr. Devlyn and Dr. Patterson, I think Mrs. Tikivik will do just fine."

Charlotte gripped the edge of the conference table, her stomach lurching with a wave of nausea. "I understand your concern, Dr. Richards. Yes, I will admit I have a close relationship with my patient, but I can assure you I will not be irrational. Are you from Nunavut originally, Dr. Richards?"

"I don't understand the point of the question. What does that have to do with this situation?"

"A lot, in fact," Dr. Patterson interjected. He sent Charlotte an encouraging look. "I think I understand what Dr. James is getting at."

"Well, I don't."

"Just answer it," Quinn said.

"No. I'm not from here. I'm from Vancouver."

"People in remote communities can be very untrusting of strangers. This territory is very close-knit, given its vastness. I've know the Tikiviks for a long time and they trust me. If you try to remove me from the O.R., it will only upset Mrs. Tikivik, possibly putting her into distress."

"Dr. James is correct. And Mrs. Tikivik is very…strong-willed," Quinn said delicately, though a hint of a smile played on his lips. "I need Dr. James to assist me. I've known her for a long time, too, and I value her skills. Dr. Richards, you are needed to monitor the fetus and take care of the child if an EXIT procedure is required. Dr. Patterson's main concern is the health of the mother."

Dr. Richards assessed Charlotte. "Your points are valid. You've swayed me and I concur."

Quinn sent a glance that conveyed his relief. Charlotte nodded and pulled out another cracker, shoving it into her mouth as Dr. Richards flipped open her notebook.

"Now, can we discuss the real reason we're here?" Quinn

clicked on his slide show and the large screen in the board-room lit up with sonograms of the fetus. "The fetus is at a gestational age of thirty weeks and, as you can tell, the lesion has grown." Quinn used a pointer to indicate the lesion. "The fetus will develop hydrops soon."

"And given Mrs. Tikivik is already a high-risk candidate, I have no doubt she'll develop mirror syndrome, which will quickly escalate into fatal pre-eclampsia," Dr. Patterson added.

"What're you suggesting, Dr. Devlyn?" Dr. Richards asked.

"We need to perform a fetal resection today."

"And that is the best course of action?" Charlotte asked. "It won't tax Mentlana, having two C-sections so close together?"

"It's the best option, Dr. James," Quinn said seriously. "The fetus will feel nothing and will have the benefit of his mother's blood supply from the placenta, a chance to heal in the womb and to let the lungs develop more. Mentlana will have to re-main in Iqaluit and be monitored for preterm labor."

Charlotte nodded. "I'll inform my patient."

Quinn turned to Dr. Patterson. "We need an O.R. prepped."

"We'll have one ready within the hour. The longer we wait, the greater the risk her blood pressure will climb." Dr. Pat-terson stood.

Charlotte got up and left the boardroom. Her heart was pounding and it felt like it was going to burst out of her chest.

You can do this. I know you can.

She could, and she would for Mentlana. She paused at the door to Mentlana's room and saw she was alone, staring at the wall. The room was still dark, but Genen and Lorna were no longer there.

When Charlotte entered the room, Mentlana looked at her, her face drawn and all the apprehension her friend had been trying to hide finally bubbling to the surface.

"Hey, Charley." Mentlana's voice wavered. "What's the verdict?"

"Where's Genen?" Charlotte asked, sitting on the edge of the bed.

"I sent him to get breakfast. Someone had to eat something around here."

Charlotte nodded. "You'll be able to eat soon."

Mentlana inhaled, her hand shaking in Charlotte's. "Tell me."

"Do you want to wait for Genen?"

"No. Tell me."

"The lesion has grown quite a bit since the last sonogram. The baby is at risk of developing heart failure and you are at risk of developing pre-eclampsia, which is fatal."

Two big fat tears rolled down Mentlana's cheeks. "Oh, God."

"We're going to do a fetal resection of the CCAM."

"What does that mean?"

"We're going to do something similar to a C-section but not deliver the baby. We'll partially delivery him, repair the lesion and place him back in your womb."

"Why don't you deliver him?"

"The idea is to try and keep him in there for as long as possible, until he's full term and we deliver him via C-section."

Mentlana's face paled. "That's the best course?"

Charlotte nodded. "Yes."

"Will the baby feel pain?"

"No." Charlotte squeezed Mentlana's hand. "This is the best course of action. Trust me."

"I do. You'll be there, right?"

"Yes. I will." Charlotte stood. "I know this is a lot to take in. Two C-sections are not ideal close together, but your baby has a better chance of survival this way."

Mentlana sighed and closed her eyes. "I'll face whatever I have to, to have my child."

"I know. I admire you for that."

Mentlana opened her eyes. "You will, too, when the time comes."

Charlotte nodded. She was beginning to believe it, but Mentlana was still something amazing and special to her. "I know physicians aren't supposed to say this to their patients, but I love you."

Mentlana grinned. "I love you, too. I'm glad you're here."

Charlotte hugged her, tears flowing. "Oh, dammit, stupid pregnancy hormones."

Mentlana laughed and brushed away her own tears. "I like seeing this side of you, Charley."

"What side?"

"The non-obstinate one."

Charlotte just shook her head. "I'll find Genen for you."

"Thanks, Charley."

Charlotte nodded and left the room. She didn't care who saw her tears, even Dr. Richards. She was done hiding her emotions.

She was done being obstinate.

CHAPTER SEVENTEEN

CHARLOTTE WATCHED QUINN scrubbing up. They were alone for the first time since she'd decided to tell him she was pregnant. She prayed she was doing the right thing, telling him before the surgery, but she couldn't keep it in any longer. She had to tell him.

"How are you feeling?" she asked, cautiously.

"Nervous, but I'm confident."

"The only fear is fear itself." She was quoting something her father had always said to her when she'd been hesitant to try new things as a child.

"Easy for you to say." He gave her a half smile, teasing her.

"I'm afraid of other things, but I'm willing to face the thing that terrifies me the most."

"What?"

"I'm afraid of carrying another child, Quinn." Tears stung her eyes. "I'd never thought of becoming a mother again, but I watched Mentlana and her trials and tribulations to have one. She was so brave, but for me the idea hurt too much. I'm still terrified, but I'll face the fear of losing it again because it's what I want."

Quinn's eyes widened, and he paused in scrubbing. "You're pregnant?"

Charlotte nodded and her knees began to knock. "I'm not

telling you this to force something from you. I can do this on my own. I want this. I just… You have the right to know."

Quinn remained frozen. "I don't know what to say."

"There's nothing to say, Quinn. You don't have to be a part of it."

"Thank you for letting me know. It's a lot to process."

"I know you're not thrilled—"

"Who says I'm not?" Quinn interrupted.

Charlotte sighed. "You weren't exactly over the moon last time. You were relieved when I lost it."

Quinn shook his head. "No, not at all. I was just as hurt as you were. I was trying to ease your pain my stupid foot-in-mouth way by hiding it. I thought by telling you about a great medical opportunity you would follow me, but I thought you were blaming me for the loss of our baby and that you hated me."

Charlotte felt the blood drain from her face. "I…I don't know what to say."

"Charlotte, you want to know my fear?"

"Of course."

"I was afraid of being a father. I didn't have the best role model to base any experience on. I was afraid of screwing up our child's life."

"Excuse me, Dr. Devlyn?" A nurse from the O.R. appeared. "We're ready for you to go over the instruments with the scrub nurse."

Quinn nodded. "Thank you."

The nurse disappeared and Quinn shook the water off his hands. "We'll talk about this later, Charlotte."

Charlotte nodded. "Of course."

He disappeared into the O.R. and she felt like she was going to faint. She felt relieved and over-the-moon happy. He'd mourned the loss of their first child just as keenly as she had.

Yes, she'd carry this child, no matter what the outcome. She wanted this baby.

Badly.

* * *

Quinn stood by the surgical table in the operating room. He was scrubbed in and ready to go. Mentlana hadn't been brought in yet, but he knew they were prepping her.

It'd been a long time since he'd been in this position. He stared at the surgical tools on the tray in front of him. Tools he was all too familiar with. He knew every nuance of them, how they functioned and at what step in the procedure he would need them, but still replayed it over and over again in his mind.

It was a way to calm and reassure himself he was capable of doing the surgery.

Steady. Just count.

He focused on the instruments—the scalpel, the sutures, the small, delicate tools he'd need to operate on such a fragile being. He flexed his fingers in the glove. There was no pain, just a bit of numbness.

Steady.

He took a deep breath. The room was chilly and the antiseptic smell calmed him. The nurses were shuffling around the room, doing their own counting as they set up the instruments, and that was reassuring.

Everything is going to be okay. I can do this.

Quinn closed his eyes and replayed in his mind the last fetal resection he'd done. The one he'd done before his accident. The baby was a healthy, thriving toddler now. Just like Mentlana's would be in a year's time.

When he thought of babies, though, his mind went to the one Charlotte was carrying. He smiled, though no one could see it behind the surgical mask. What if Charlotte was going to be on this table and it was their child's life in another surgeon's hands or his own? How would he deal with it? He had to be at the top of his game. He wouldn't let Genen down.

This baby was going to survive. His hand wasn't going to spasm.

I will succeed.

"Are you all right, Dr. Devlyn?" the scrub nurse asked cautiously, as she began to lay out the instruments in order.

"I am, thank you..."

"Bernice."

"Bernice. Good. I do like to know the name of my scrub nurse. Have you attended a surgery like this before?"

The nurse nodded. "At SickKids in Toronto."

Quinn's eyes widened. "This isn't where you work?"

Bernice shook her head. "No. I'm from Toronto and came as a favor to Dr. James. She said you needed a scrub nurse who'd assisted surgeons in this procedure before."

Quinn exhaled, relief oozing out of his very pores as the tension in his shoulders dissipated and he loosened up. Charlotte had done this for him? Any lingering concern he had vanished in that moment. With a good scrub nurse he'd be able to focus on the task at hand and not worry about instructing some other nurse on what he needed and when. Bernice would instinctively know what to hand him at each stage.

"I could kiss Dr. James right about now. I'd kiss you, too."

"You can't tamper with the sterilized field, Dr. Devlyn." Bernice chuckled, her eyes twinkling above her surgical mask. "I really don't fancy scrubbing in again, but I do appreciate your enthusiasm for my presence." Bernice moved off to continue her preparations.

I can do this.

The doors to the operating room slid open and Dr. Patterson entered the room. The nurses slipped on his gloves and Quinn nodded in greeting to the obstetrician.

Ready to do this again.

"It's time." Charlotte stepped aside as the orderlies wheeled the gurney in the room. Genen looked nauseous and worried. It broke Charlotte's heart, but she couldn't let her emotions take hold of her right now. At least her own nausea had subsided, thanks to some Diclectin that Dr. Patterson had given her a few hours ago when she'd approached him about morning sickness. Each pregnancy was *supposed* to be different, but again she was being plagued with horrible morning sickness. You'd think the odds would be in her favor.

Of course, she didn't want to think about the odds right now. If she did she'd only dwell on the statistics, which weren't in Mentlana's favor right now. Charlotte took a deep breath, trying to take Lorna's advice to heart. She was trying not to worry about a bad outcome, and to think on a good one. Though it was hard to break a habit of a lifetime when you kept getting dealt a rotten hand most of the time, and had to work for every little thing.

Mentlana and her baby would survive.

She had to believe it. For the first time in her life she had to believe in more than medical science. She had to put her trust and her hope in faith.

Mentlana and Genen kissed, which tugged at her heartstrings. The orderlies lifted Mentlana onto the gurney while her nurses began to hang the IV bags and catheter.

"Genen, you can walk us down the hall," Charlotte offered. "But because she's going under general anaesthesia, you can't come into the theater."

"I want to be with her," Genen protested.

"I know you do, but you can't. When we deliver the baby at the end of her pregnancy, you can. She'll have a spinal then and be wide awake. Trust me. It's for the best you wait out here, Genen."

Genen nodded and held tightly to Mentlana's hand as the orderlies wheeled the gurney out of the room. Charlotte followed beside them as they whisked Mentlana off to the operating suites. They stopped at the double doors and Charlotte moved away, pulling Genen to the side as Mentlana disappeared.

"You can't go any farther, Genen. I'm sorry."

Genen was visibly shaking, his dark eyes moist with tears. "Please, take care of her, Doc."

"Of course I will…I promise." Although she never promised any patient, the words just slipped past her lips and she prayed that she'd be able to honor that promise.

Genen nodded and Charlotte went through the double doors into the surgical suites. Her stomach twisted in a knot as she tied back her hair and scrubbed her hands. Through the window she could see Mentlana was already laid out on the table, the lights dimmed save for the bright surgical light.

Mentlana's face was pale as she stared at the ceiling, terrified. Charlotte glanced at Quinn, who appeared calm as he chatted to the scrub nurse from SickKids.

Bernice was an old friend and a bit of a present from Dr. Harriet Preston, who'd suggested Charlotte call Quinn when she'd first discovered the lesions on Mentlana's fetus.

"You know who the best in that field is, Charley. I don't have to tell you."

She hadn't wanted to call Quinn, but Harriet had been right. He *was* the best and now she was so glad she'd screwed up her courage and called him.

Once she'd finished scrubbing, she entered the O.R. and was gloved. She headed over to Mentlana's side.

"It's going to be okay, Lana."

"Charley?" There was relief in her voice. "Is Genen okay?"

"He's fine."

"Good." Dr. Patterson began to wash Mentlana's swollen abdomen with Betadine. "Ugh, what's he doing down there, painting a fence or something?"

Dr. Patterson chuckled. "I'm quite adept at fence-painting, too, Mrs. Tikivik, though don't tell my wife."

"I like you, Dr. Patterson." Mentlana grinned, but her lips quivered. "I'm scared, Charley, so scared."

"It'll be okay, Lana. I promise."

"What if…?" Mentlana trailed off and then shook her head.

"No what-ifs. It'll be okay. Trust me."

Mentlana nodded. "I do. I trust you with every fiber of my

being and I trust Dr. Devlyn because you do. You do trust him, don't you, Charley?"

"I do. He's the best."

Mentlana sighed. "I'm ready."

"Are you ready, Dr. Devlyn, Dr. Patterson?" the anesthesiologist asked.

"Yes," Quinn replied, his voice steady and calm, which reassured Charlotte. "Ready when you are, Dr. Horne."

Dr. Horne stepped forward. "We're going to put you under now, Mrs. Tikivik." A nurse placed an oxygen mask over Mentlana's face while Dr. Horne injected something into her IV line. "Just breathe deeply, Mrs. Tikivik. Good. Now start to count back from one hundred, please."

Charlotte left Mentlana's side as she counted, each number sounding more and more slurred. She stood beside Quinn.

"How are you feeling?" Quinn whispered.

"Fine. Dr. Patterson gave me something for nausea, but I'm ready to assist. How are you?"

"Excellent. This will be a success, Charlotte."

"Do you promise?"

"I never promise."

Charlotte bit her lip. "I know you can't."

He leaned over and whispered, "Off the record, I do. I promise."

"The patient is sedated," Dr. Horne said.

"All right, ladies and gentleman, let's proceed." Dr. Patterson stepped forward to perform the incision. "Ten blade."

Charlotte watched in wonder and amazement as Dr. Patterson skillfully operated on Mentlana, exposing her uterus and cutting into it. It'd been a long time since she'd assisted in surgery and she'd forgotten what a thrill it was, but she wouldn't trade this thrill for the high she got by dealing with her patients every day.

Often she wondered if she'd done the right thing by turning down a residency as a surgeon and entering general practice, but standing here and knowing every aspect of Mentlana's medical history, whereas these specialized surgeons only knew snippets, made Charlotte realize she'd made the right choice. Charlotte knew everything about her patients. She knew and understood the whole picture, and for that she was thankful.

"We're ready now, Dr. Devlyn." Dr. Patterson stepped back.

Charlotte looked at Quinn and nodded. *You can do this, Quinn.* She hoped she conveyed everything she wanted to say to him in a single look as he moved into position and began the fetal resection.

She stood by his side, waiting to see if she'd be needed, but he didn't ask her for help. His hands were fluid and gentle as he carefully lifted the baby out of Mentlana's abdomen and began the surgery to remove the lesion.

"Amazing," Dr. Richards whispered behind Charlotte. She glanced over her shoulder to see the pediatric specialist watching Quinn with total hero-worship.

Charlotte grinned in admiration at the man she loved, handling the baby so gently. The procedure flew by. He'd been so terrified that he'd need her, that he'd hurt or kill the baby, but he'd had nothing to worry about. All Charlotte did was hold the retractor and Bernice handed him the instruments he required.

"Damn," Quinn cursed.

The blood drained out of Charlotte's face as he paused, the baby resting in his hand.

"Dr. Devlyn?" Bernice questioned.

Quinn shot Charlotte a look.

"Cramp?" she asked.

"Yes." There was tension in his voice.

"Are you okay, Dr. Devlyn?" Patterson asked.

"Perfectly. My stamina is the worse for wear, but if Dr. James assists me, I should be fine. I'm almost finished."

Charlotte nodded. "Dr. Richards, please hold the retractor for me."

Dr. Richards stepped forward and she slipped her hand over

Charlotte's, taking the retractor without moving it and applying the same pressure Charlotte had been using.

Charlotte gently gripped Quinn's hand. The muscles were taut, and she began to palpate the palm, easing the muscles.

"You can do it," she said under her breath, encouraging him.

Quinn nodded and finished the resection. Charlotte stared down at the almost-full-term baby. Though he had ten weeks to go, he was beautiful, with the start of a full crop of thick black hair and some baby fat was beginning to flesh out his limbs. The baby's body was still covered in protective lanugo. Tears stung her eyes as she looked into that tiny, precious face. Mentlana and Genen's whole world, being held in Quinn's healing hands.

Live.

"There," Quinn announced, relief and joy in his voice. "Help me place the fetus back in the womb, Dr. James."

"Of course." She cupped her hands underneath Quinn's and they gently placed the baby back in his mother's uterus.

"Amazing," Dr. Richards whispered again in awe.

"It is." Quinn's gaze locked with Charlotte's just for a brief moment. As they placed the baby back in utero the baby's arm shot out of the incision and latched onto Quinn's finger, squeezing it.

A sob caught in Charlotte's throat as she watched the baby in amazement. The tiny infant was reaching out for human contact and comfort.

"Will you…?" Quinn's voice shook. "Help me, Charlotte."

She brushed the little hand off Quinn's finger, despite its firm grip, and set it back in place.

"She's all yours, Dr. Patterson," Quinn said, stepping back.

"Thank you, Dr. Devlyn. Okay, let's get Mrs. Tikivik closed. Zero Vicryl, please, Bernice."

Quinn walked away from Mentlana towards the scrub room. His job was done. Charlotte didn't follow but remained by Mentlana's side. She was confident Dr. Patterson and Dr. Richards would be able to handle the rest of the surgery expertly, but she'd promised her friend that she wouldn't leave.

Charlotte glanced over towards the scrub room. She wanted to follow Quinn, wanted to hold him in her arms and thank him for saving her friend's life, but that would come later. She moved around to Mentlana's head. The anesthesiologist was monitoring the machines and Charlotte pulled over a rolling stool and sat by her friend. Ignoring the tube that helped Mentlana breathe and her taped eyes, she stroked her friend's hair, hoping Mentlana could sense her presence.

"Everything's all right, Lana," she whispered. "The baby is fine."

And I'll be fine, too.

CHAPTER EIGHTEEN

QUINN KNEW CHARLOTTE couldn't follow him out. He knew she'd be faithful and remain by Mentlana's side, but right now he could use her. He needed to see her friendly face and share in the joy that was surging through him.

I did it.

His hands shook as he leaned against the cold tiled wall of the scrub room. He peeled the rubber gloves from his hands, disposed of them and then removed the surgical gown and stuffed it into the laundry bin, followed by his scrub cap.

His knees were wobbly as he pressed his foot against the bar, allowing the water in the scrub sink to rush over his skin without having to touch anything. Quinn glanced down at his hands, his broken one and the scars that crisscrossed his skin, scars he'd been ashamed of. They no longer bothered him.

They represented a point in his life he'd rather forget and wished had never happened. The memory of the accident that had almost cost him his life would remain with him, but the crash would no longer haunt him. Anything life could throw at him was not insurmountable, not with Charlotte by his side.

In that moment when the baby had reached out and curled his hand around his finger, squeezing him to let him know he was there and alive, had been a miracle.

Never in his years as a fetal surgeon had he ever experienced such a moment, such an affirmation of life.

A life he'd saved.

He'd survived the accident that had damaged his hand, when so many hadn't. He was lucky he had been given a second chance, at surgery and at a future with Charlotte.

Quinn scrubbed his hands. He'd been terrified at the prospect of this moment, but had kept it to himself.

Now there was one more life he had to save.

His own.

There was no way he was going to allow Charlotte to walk out of his life again because they couldn't agree to practice medicine in the same place. Quinn was not going to make the same mistake twice.

He was lucky she hadn't moved on, that she was still single and wanted him. He wasn't going to tempt fate. This time the odds were in his favor. The fates were smiling on him and he was going to make everything right.

Quinn left the O.R. suites. First he'd find Genen and update him on his wife and child and then he was going to make some changes.

It was time to stop being so selfish.

It was time to live.

"Where am I?"

Charlotte straightened and leaned over Mentlana's bed in the recovery room. She took her friend's hand and rubbed it gently. Mentlana was still groggy. They'd woken her in the O.R. after the surgery was complete, but she hadn't been quite awake after several general nudges.

Charlotte remained by her bedside in Recovery, wanting to tell Mentlana herself that her son would be fine.

"Where am I?" Mentlana asked again.

"Recovery."

"Charley?"

"I'm here." Charlotte smiled as Mentlana's eyes fluttered open.

"Thank you for staying with me." Mentlana's eyes closed again.

"Don't fall asleep again. You need to stay awake." Charlotte stood and gestured to one of the nurses. "They're going to check on you, okay?"

"Don't go, Charley. Please."

"I promise I won't."

Charlotte stepped back so the recovery-room nurses could check Mentlana's vitals, the baby's vitals and the incision, but she stayed where Mentlana could see her. The effects of the anesthesia were wearing off. Charlotte watched as Mentlana came out of her haze of medication.

"I'll be back again in ten minutes, Dr. James," the nurse said as she drew the curtain around Mentlana. Charlotte sat back down.

"How's the pain?" she asked, rubbing Mentlana's leg.

She winced, her face pale. "Not pleasant, but the nurse shot some morphine into my butt."

Charlotte grinned. "You should be feeling good in a few minutes."

Mentlana nodded. "So tell me. I'm ready to hear whatever you have to say, good or bad."

"All good," Charlotte whispered, barely containing her glee.

Mentlana perked up, more alert. "What?"

"Dr. Devlyn corrected the baby's CCAM. If we can keep him inside you for a bit longer and get him closer to term, everything should be okay."

Tears began to roll down Mentlana's face, and her shoulders shook as she reached out and grasped Charlotte's arm. "It hurts to cry."

Charlotte tried to swallow the lump in her throat but couldn't, and soon she was weeping in joy along with her friend.

"Thank you," Mentlana said, wiping away the tears with the back of her hand.

"You're welcome."

"You thank Quinn, too." Mentlana closed her eyes, tears still streaming. "I don't even know how to begin to thank him."

"You'll find a way." Charlotte's voice was still wobbly and she cleared her throat to regain her composure. "Why don't you make him a great big honking plate of muktuk?"

Mentlana grinned. "Perhaps I should, but I think he'd rather receive my thanks through you. He didn't come up here because he's a humanitarian, Charley. If you were just any old physician he wouldn't have come. He would've found another one or I would've had to fly to Toronto and break the bank to do it. The reason he came up here, at his own expense, was you."

Warmth crept up Charlotte's neck. Mentlana spoke the truth. Quinn loved her and she loved him. "Still, I think he has a certain fondness for you, Mentlana."

"Good. Or I'd have to kick him in that soft spot I spoke of before." Mentlana winked. "Don't let him get away, Charley. Don't let him walk away from you and that precious bundle you carry. Even if it means you have to leave us in Cape Recluse and head to the bright lights of the city."

"I won't." Charlotte stood. "I know I'll have to leave here to live in Toronto. I'll miss you."

"And I you, but you can always visit. You do know how to fly."

Charlotte laughed and stroked Mentlana's face affectionately. "The nurses are going to give me heck for getting you all emotionally riled up."

A devilish grin spread across Mentlana's face. "I'll tell them where to go. You helped save my baby. You and Dr. Devlyn have given me everything I've ever wanted."

Charlotte kissed her forehead. "Rest. I'll see you later."

"Tell him, Charley. Tell him and don't let him go."

Charlotte nodded and left the recovery room. Her heart

was singing with joy as she walked down the corridor of the hospital with a spring in her step.

Tell him, Charley. Tell him and don't let him go. Mentlana's words were weighing on her. Her friend had never been so right. For five years she'd waited and mourned the loss of their baby and the loss of Quinn.

Now he was back in her life and she was pregnant again. She'd do anything to keep Quinn in her life, even if it meant leaving the North and moving to the city, be it Toronto, Manhattan or Abu Dhabi. Charlotte didn't care. She just wanted Quinn.

She had to be flexible and not so stubborn.

Charlotte's hand drifted down over her abdomen and she thought about the little life just starting out in her womb. She meant to go and find Quinn, tell him how she felt and how she was willing to go anywhere, risk everything to be with him.

This was for the best. Her baby needed a father. She'd finally have the family she'd always dreamed of since she'd lost her parents.

She also needed Quinn. Charlotte was aware of that now. She couldn't live without him.

Her phone buzzed and she pulled it out. Quinn had texted her, asking her to meet him in the on-call room on the fourth floor.

A heavy weight had been lifted from her shoulders and right now she was going to make everything right. She wasn't going to let Quinn Devlyn get away. She was going to show him exactly what he meant to her and she hoped he'd feel the same.

The on-call door was open and she slipped inside the room. When she entered, Quinn was seated on a cot, his elbows resting on his knees as he stared at a small box in his hands. He looked down at it, seeming sad and puzzled. What did he have to be sad about? He should be rejoicing. Two lives had been saved. A miracle had been performed, thanks to him.

Charlotte crossed the room and sat down next to him, placing her hand on his knee.

"Quinn, are you all right?"

He gazed at her and smiled. "Of course."

Charlotte let out a sigh of relief. "I thought you were upset."

He shook his head. "Fine. I'm fine. How's Mentlana?"

"Sore, but very grateful." Charlotte kissed his cheek. "You did it. You kept your promise to me."

"My hands cramped, but I did it. With your help."

"They're healed. I hope this outcome gives you more confidence."

"It gives me a bit." He grinned.

"It should give you more than a bit, Quinn. You're a surgeon, a surgical god again. Unfortunately, our outcomes are not always what we want or expect, but if we don't try…if we don't try to save a life, that's the real crime."

Quinn leaned over and kissed her, a tender kiss that brought tears to her eyes. He stroked her face. "I'm ready to come back from my sabbatical."

Charlotte's heart skipped a beat, her stomach churned. He was going to return to surgery, but *where* was the big question. Wherever it was, she'd follow him. She was ready, as much as she hated living in the city.

"What's wrong?" he asked, confused. "Look, I know you don't want to live in the city…"

"No. I'm certain of what I want, too."

"Certain of what?"

"That I can leave here to follow you." She ran her fingers along his jaw, the stubble tickling her fingertips. "I'll go wherever you need to. Wherever you want to."

"You don't have to leave. You belong up here. This is your home."

"Quinn, you're my life now. Wherever you are, I'm home. I won't lose you."

"You won't. I was made an offer by this hospital to be the

head of the neonatal unit. They want a state-of-the-art facil-ity here and I'm the surgeon they want to lead that project. I accepted, Charlotte."

Charlotte was floored. Her mouth dropped open. She knew she must look like a gaping fish by the way Quinn started to laugh. "You…you what?"

"I'm head of the up-and-coming new neonatal unit. Hon-estly, Charlotte, how hard can that be to understand?" He was teasing her.

"What about your chief of surgery position in Toronto? The one your father groomed you for?"

He shrugged his shoulders. "My life is with you and your life is here. You wouldn't be happy in Toronto, in close prox-imity to my mother."

"I thought you hated the North. The cold? The ice?"

"I did, but that was the old me. I'll grow used to the cold, and there are other aspects I love, but the most important draw is you, Charlotte. Besides, there are always vacations." Quinn stood and pulled her into his arms. "I love you, Charlotte. If it wasn't for you, I wouldn't be so damn happy again."

"And I love you."

"I do have one condition, though, and it does involve a city."

Charlotte cocked an eyebrow. "Oh?"

"You need to find another physician for Cape Recluse. I need my wife in Iqaluit with me."

"Deal." Charlotte kissed him, lightly brushing her lips against his.

Charlotte knew there was no way she was going to be able to hold back her tears. She was getting everything she wanted. Cape Recluse wasn't too far away that she couldn't keep an eye on it from Iqaluit—she could easily open a practice in the city. All she wanted was Quinn. She wouldn't be obstinate. He was sacrificing big money and the metropolitan way of life for her.

"If it wasn't for you, Dr. Devlyn, I wouldn't have a chance at motherhood again. I love you."

Quinn stepped back and held out the box. "I know I couldn't afford one before, being in med school and all."

Charlotte took the box and opened it. The sparkle of a diamond took her breath away. "Oh, my God."

"It's a diamond from a mine up here. I was assured of that. I wanted you to have a stone that came from the land you love."

"Quinn, it's beautiful."

He took her hand and slipped the ring on her finger. "Marry me, right away. Tomorrow even. We've waited long enough and I can't wait even a second longer. I don't want to waste any more time."

Charlotte wrapped her arms around him. "Yes, I'll marry you as soon as possible. I've waited a long time for this moment."

Quinn grinned and slipped his hand into her hair, dragging her into another toe-curling kiss.

"Shall we go visit Mentlana and Genen and bask in their happiness?" he asked breathlessly a few moments later.

"I'd like that."

They kissed one more time and walked out of the on-call suite hand in hand, with the future ahead of them.

There was no place in their world for obstinate people. Charlotte knew beyond a shadow of a doubt she'd always fight for Quinn, their family and the love they'd been given again.

Always.

* * * * *

Mills & Boon® Hardback
September 2013

ROMANCE

Challenging Dante	Lynne Graham
Captivated by Her Innocence	Kim Lawrence
Lost to the Desert Warrior	Sarah Morgan
His Unexpected Legacy	Chantelle Shaw
Never Say No to a Caffarelli	Melanie Milburne
His Ring Is Not Enough	Maisey Yates
A Reputation to Uphold	Victoria Parker
A Whisper of Disgrace	Sharon Kendrick
If You Can't Stand the Heat...	Joss Wood
Maid of Dishonour	Heidi Rice
Bound by a Baby	Kate Hardy
In the Line of Duty	Ami Weaver
Patchwork Family in the Outback	Soraya Lane
Stranded with the Tycoon	Sophie Pembroke
The Rebound Guy	Fiona Harper
Greek for Beginners	Jackie Braun
A Child to Heal Their Hearts	Dianne Drake
Sheltered by Her Top-Notch Boss	Joanna Neil

MEDICAL

The Wife He Never Forgot	Anne Fraser
The Lone Wolf's Craving	Tina Beckett
Re-awakening His Shy Nurse	Annie Claydon
Safe in His Hands	Amy Ruttan

0813 GEN STD HB

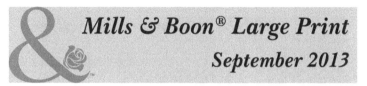

ROMANCE

A Rich Man's Whim	Lynne Graham
A Price Worth Paying?	Trish Morey
A Touch of Notoriety	Carole Mortimer
The Secret Casella Baby	Cathy Williams
Maid for Montero	Kim Lawrence
Captive in his Castle	Chantelle Shaw
Heir to a Dark Inheritance	Maisey Yates
Anything but Vanilla...	Liz Fielding
A Father for Her Triplets	Susan Meier
Second Chance with the Rebel	Cara Colter
First Comes Baby...	Michelle Douglas

HISTORICAL

The Greatest of Sins	Christine Merrill
Tarnished Amongst the Ton	Louise Allen
The Beauty Within	Marguerite Kaye
The Devil Claims a Wife	Helen Dickson
The Scarred Earl	Elizabeth Beacon

MEDICAL

NYC Angels: Redeeming The Playboy	Carol Marinelli
NYC Angels: Heiress's Baby Scandal	Janice Lynn
St Piran's: The Wedding!	Alison Roberts
Sydney Harbour Hospital: Evie's Bombshell	Amy Andrews
The Prince Who Charmed Her	Fiona McArthur
His Hidden American Beauty	Connie Cox

Mills & Boon® Hardback
October 2013

ROMANCE

The Greek's Marriage Bargain	Sharon Kendrick
An Enticing Debt to Pay	Annie West
The Playboy of Puerto Banús	Carol Marinelli
Marriage Made of Secrets	Maya Blake
Never Underestimate a Caffarelli	Melanie Milburne
The Divorce Party	Jennifer Hayward
A Hint of Scandal	Tara Pammi
A Façade to Shatter	Lynn Raye Harris
Whose Bed Is It Anyway?	Natalie Anderson
Last Groom Standing	Kimberly Lang
Single Dad's Christmas Miracle	Susan Meier
Snowbound with the Soldier	Jennifer Faye
The Redemption of Rico D'Angelo	Michelle Douglas
The Christmas Baby Surprise	Shirley Jump
Backstage with Her Ex	Louisa George
Blame It on the Champagne	Nina Harrington
Christmas Magic in Heatherdale	Abigail Gordon
The Motherhood Mix-Up	Jennifer Taylor

MEDICAL

Gold Coast Angels: A Doctor's Redemption	Marion Lennox
Gold Coast Angels: Two Tiny Heartbeats	Fiona McArthur
The Secret Between Them	Lucy Clark
Craving Her Rough Diamond Doc	Amalie Berlin

0913 GEN STD HB

Mills & Boon® Large Print
October 2013

ROMANCE

HISTORICAL

MEDICAL